D0847965

GUNFIGHTER'S RETURN

GUNFIGHTER'S RETURN

Leslie Ernenwein

GUNSMOKE

This hardback edition 2009
by BBC Audiobooks Ltd
by arrangement with
Golden West Literary Agency

ISBN 978 1 405 68238 1

British Library Cataloguing in Publication Data available.

Printed and bound in Great Britain by
CPI Antony Rowe, Chippenham, Wiltshire

CHAPTER ONE

Durango died at noon. He didn't say a word. Didn't even grunt. He just lay down and died.

This was the Rio Soledad, fifty horseback miles from San Sebastian. Here, on a sun-cracked parchment of baked mud crusting the dry river bed, Jim Rimbaud stood holding a bloody bandage he had been adjusting for Durango. Fatigue slouched Rimbaud's lean-shanked body; it marked his angular face and was a dullness in his eyes. Beyond him, propped on trembling legs, stood two tired horses. Perspiration lathered their heaving flanks and ran from their bellies like rain dripping off the eaves of a barn.

Rimbaud peered down at Durango's slack-jawed face and remembered how this dead man had dreamed of becoming *presidente* of all Mexico. He had even planned a new flag for the republic—a red and white freedom flag shaped like a calvary guidon. A great dreamer, Durango, and a great fighter. But he'd had one weakness. Women. Sprawly, sweet-smelling women. Tall or short, lean or lardy, Durango had taken his women where he found them. And one, a swivel-hipped cantina dancer with no more morals than a mare in heat, had betrayed him for a pouch of federal gold. Durango didn't look like a brave general of *insurrectos* now. He looked like a lazy peon taking a siesta with a belly full of beans.

A cynical smile rutted Rimbaud's whisker-shagged cheeks as he dropped the bloody bandage at Durango's side. "There's your freedom flag," he muttered. "Red and white, just like you planned."

Then he faced southward, observing a long smear of risen dust above the barren plain. That would be the federal cavalry coming to do the job it had failed to accomplish last night at San Sebastian. For even though the *federalistas* had slaughtered scores of screaming rebels and wounded countless others, including Durango, they hadn't captured the two men Diaz sought above all others—General Francisco Durango and his American accomplice.

It was characteristic of Jim Rimbaud that he didn't glance at Durango again. The smoky years had given him a gambler's fatalism. Durango was dead. Finished. And so was his fabulous dream of driving Porfirio Diaz from the *palacio nacional*. There had been some chance of winning the revolution while Durango lived, but now there was no chance at all. For Francisco had been the sturdy thong that bound a rebel horde together. Without him the *insurrectos* would scatter like quail into the brush.

Calculating the distance between this dry river bed and the oncoming riders, Rimbaud decided that it was not more than three miles. A matter of minutes. A man couldn't make a stand here. Nor anywhere this side of the border hills. The land was smooth as the palm of a pimp's hand. Rimbaud plodded over to the horses in the slow-motion way of a man too tired for faster movement, and gave the downheaded animals a squint-eyed appraisal. There seemed little choice between them, for they were both close to being foundered.

"Wore out," Rimbaud muttered, "like me."

As a shadow darted across the sunlit dust he

peered up at a buzzard that circled patiently on tilted wings. Soon there would be more of the desert scavengers. Rimbaud wondered who would reach Durango first, the *federalistas* or the buzzards. He shrugged, thinking it would make no difference to Durango.

Moving without hurry, Rimbaud untied Durango's saddlebags and transferred them to his rat-tailed roan gelding. The cavalry, he supposed, had obtained fresh horses from some friendly hacienda this morning. There would be no chance of the roan's outrunning them to the border hills, which were upwards of fifteen miles away. Yet, because he possessed a thorough knowledge of his pursuers, Rimbaud retained a cynical confidence. The power of gringo gold was great in Mexico. It might buy him the time he needed to reach those hills.

So thinking, Rimbaud rode north, prodding the reluctant roan to a slow trot. Durango's jaded horse nickered once and took a faltering step forward. But its reins were down and weariness was an added deterrent, so it remained there, ignoring the green-bellied flies and the buzzards that came down in patient circling.

Rimbaud glanced rearward occasionally, tallied the oncoming riders as being ten in number, and saw that they were steadily gaining on him. Presently he opened the flap of a saddlebag and brought out a handful of gold pieces—American double eagles, which in Mexico were worth five times their face value. He dropped one to the ground, and seeing how brightly it shone in the sunlight, understood the temptation it would be to poorly paid *soldados*. Gold was like a passionate woman wanting to be possessed; a smiling, warm-eyed woman with her arms open. He tossed a gold piece to the left of the roan's tracks and another

7

one to the right, then flipped two more farther out on each side.

Oro de Libertad, Durango had called it; gold for the liberation. A small fortune of it. Jim Rimbaud smiled thinly, hoping that the double eagles would last long enough to liberate a gringo drifter whose sole ambition was to reach Arizona Territory alive. A greedy man might have sowed the gold pieces sparingly and with tight-fingered reluctance; might have flinched at relinquishing this last chance to reap reward for risking his hide below the border. But not Jim Rimbaud. He dropped the double eagles gladly, eagerly, fashioning golden barriers behind him. Or so he hoped. . . .

Keeping a watch rearward, Rimbaud wondered if his pursuers had reached the first spread of glinting gold pieces. They were past Durango now, for he'd seen the two leaders dismount and examine the body. It was difficult to judge the exact location of the gold pieces from this distance, but it seemed to Rimbaud that his pursuers must be very close to it. And presently, seeing no alteration in the oncoming group, he decided that they had passed the first batch of double eagles.

Wearily, in the fatalistic fashion of a gambler who had bet his last blue chip and must abide the outcome, Rimbaud watched those distance-dwarfed shapes ride toward him. He was convinced now that they had passed the first gold pieces. But they hadn't stopped.

"Odd," Rimbaud mused. "Goddamn odd."

One double eagle was worth more than three months' pay for a *soldado*. It would purchase gallons of tequila and the prettiest girl in the *congal* district. But those bandoleered bastards weren't stopping.

Apprehension replaced Rimbaud's surprise. He spurred the roan to a floundering run. He peered at the heat-hazed hills ahead and knew his tired mount wouldn't last to reach them. At a walk, yes. But not at a run.

Rimbaud drew his pistol from its holster, thinking that he would rather take a bullet here than standing with his back to an adobe wall. Better to go down fighting than to wait with your guts churning like a sweat-drenched chump caught short in a poker game. Fatigue and futility closed in like nagging companions, having their dismal way with him. This, he reflected, was what being sorry for the underdogs got you—a chance to die alone in the Sonora dust. Durango's insurrection had seemed like a grand crusade six months ago; an open invitation to fighting men who wanted to strike a blow for freedom. But it had been a futile undertaking; futile as this slow-motion flight.

Rimbaud looked back, curious to know how close the cavalry was, and could scarcely believe his eyes. The group had pulled up. One man was already on the ground. Now another dismounted, and another. They were all quitting their saddles!

Jim Rimbaud loosed a gusty sigh. "*Oro de Libertad*," he breathed, and holstered his gun.

For a time then, while he kept the roan to a shuffling jog, Rimbaud watched his backtrail. The cavalry was farther off each time he looked, the lead riders stopping to pick up gold pieces while rear ones raced on to the next nest of glittering double eagles.

"Like hogs hunting acorns," Rimbaud mused derisively, and flung another handful, spreading the gold of liberation wide, as a man sowing seed on fertile ground.

Afternoon's slanting sunlight was furnace hot now, a scorching, biting heat that sucked moisture from Rimbaud's body so that sweat stains on his shirt dried to a white salt rime. He'd had no water

9

since shortly after daybreak: no food since yesterday, and no sleep. He took a cartridge from his belt and put it in his mouth, the warm metal inducing a slight moisture of saliva. But there was nothing he could do about the hunger grind in his belly.

Rimbaud tilted the brim of his dust-peppered hat low over his aching eyes. He contemplated the border hills, estimating the miles at nine or ten. There was a spring due north on the southern slope; Smuggler's Well, they called it. And the town of Junction lay a few miles beyond the divide in Quadrille Basin. He had once spent a month in Junction, recovering from a bullet-slashed tendon in his left leg. Thinking back to that occasion, Rimbaud tallied the date and was surprised that it had been scarcely two years ago. He had done a lot of drifting since then, and a hell-smear of fighting.

"Too goddamn much," he muttered, and saw himself for what he was: a cynical drifter disillusioned by lost causes. At twenty-eight his chief possessions were a Buntline model revolver and a worn-out horse. That, plus a puckered scar where a bullet had gouged his right cheek, and another scar on his thigh, was ten years of freelance fighting had got him.

Softly, in the way of a man making a solemn vow, Rimbaud said, "I've had enough, by God. More than aplenty."

Afterward, rousing from a spell of near dozing, he sowed another spread of gold pieces. The saddlebags were almost empty now. But the border hills were much closer; they lay huddled in the shimmering heat haze like dusty elephants asleep in the sunlight. The Arizona-Sonora line ran across the base of them, which was as far as the Mexican cavalry would come. If the roan remained on his feet for another hour he would be stirring the dust of American soil.

A good place to be, Rimbaud reflected, thinking of other gringo drifters who'd been 'dobe-walled back yonder. A man was a goddamn fool to get mixed up with underdogs. Might made right. The *federalistas* had proved that at San Sebastian. They had known just where and when to strike, thanks to Durango's itch for that swivel-rumped cantina slut. Remembering how it had been, with Durango's ragged rebels outnumbered ten to one, Rimbaud grimaced, and considered himself fortunate to be alive.

When finally he came to the hills, Rimbaud halted and scanned the plain behind him. The cavalry was a long way off now, strung-out dots below a greasy rag of dust. "*Adios*," he called, and was mildly surprised at the croaking tone of his voice. It sounded, he thought, like the creaking of rusty hinges on a corral gate. Riding up the first brush-tangled slant of the hills, he took his bearings and chose a pass that should lead to Smuggler's Well, and hoped it would.

It did.

Near sundown Rimbaud lay full length in hoof-packed mud and drank cheek to cheek with his horse. American mud and American water. The luke-warm liquid was rank from recent tromping of range cattle, but no water had ever tasted better to Jim Rimbaud. It reminded him of an opinion Durango had expressed this morning while he sucked the seepage out of cow tracks in a dry river bed: "The goodness of water is in thirst, *amigo*."

A queer cuss, Durango. The son of a wealthy landowner, he had risen to a position of power second only to Diaz. Yet he had been so filled with pity for the downtrodden peons that he turned his back on the well-fed aristocracy. A true Robin Hood, he had raided the rich to feed the poor and won the highest acclaim a man could achieve:

bandido terrifico! All the poor ones had rallied to his call. Even the women, for Durango had been like a ridge-running stud attracting mares from far distances.

Rimbaud lay there pleasantly relaxed, remembering how it had been with Durango. The mud's welcome dampness soaked through his clothing, and the water had lessened his hunger. He took another drink, washed his face, and said amusedly, "Now all I need is a shave and haircut."

Presently he investigated the saddlebags and found seven double eagles remaining: a hundred and forty dollars. There had been upwards of two thousand dollars' worth of them at noon, which was the approximate price he had paid for the privilege of living.

"Cheap," Rimbaud said. Pocketing the seven gold pieces, he added, "Enough for a celebration in Junction town," and wondered if Eve Odegarde still ran her little restaurant next door to Gabbert's Livery. Remembering how womanly and appealing and self-sufficient she had been, Rimbaud grinned. There, by God, was a woman. A real, double-breasted, female woman. Every hot-blooded bachelor in Junction had made a try at courting her, without success. She had seemed surprised because he didn't, and had mentioned it once in roundabout fashion. But he had understood that she would accept nothing less than marriage, and a wife was the last thing he'd wanted. Thinking back to the night he left Junction, Rimbaud recalled that Eve Odegarde had wished him luck and said soberly, "A drifter finds only trouble, no matter how far he rides."

Well, her prediction had been correct. He'd found trouble aplenty these past two years, and damned little else. . . .

A three-quarter moon had risen above the rim of

Quadrille Basin when Rimbaud angled into the stage road west of Junction. The smell of disturbed dust came faintly to him. He scanned the moonlit road, expecting to see sign of recent travel, and was surprised at not finding it. Pulling up, Rimbaud listened, and noticed that the road cut through an upthrust of shelving rock directly ahead. Manzanita darkly shadowed the high banks and he thought: A perfect place for ambush.

Then he laughed at himself for being spooky as a booger-hunting bronc seeing things to shy at. Hell, this wasn't Sonora. The dust he'd smelled had probably been raised by a band of horses heading for water through some nearby wash. So thinking, he rode on into the defile.

Jim Rimbaud didn't see the loop that darted down from above him. He heard it swish past his ears, then felt the rope bite both arms as it yanked him headlong from the saddle. He was trying to get a hand up for protection when the ground exploded against his face.

For a brief, blank interval Rimbaud felt nothing at all. Then he became remotely aware of voices, of being lifted, and of being dropped. Afterward he understood that he was lying face down in the road. Blood and dust made a gritty mixture in his mouth, and there was a throbbing ache along his left temple. Turning over, he supported himself on an elbow and peered about him. The roan stood cropping grass a dozen yards south of the highway, that methodical crunching the only sound. It occured to Rimbaud that he wasn't in the defile; glancing at the dust, he saw boot tracks where two men had carried him out here.

Still dazed by the impact of his headlong fall, Rimbaud got slowly to his feet. Noticing that his holster was empty, he muttered, "So are my pockets—and my belly." He wondered if the bandits had left him enough to buy supper, and was astonished to find the seven gold pieces along with some silver coins in his pocket.

That baffled Jim Rimbaud. Why had they waylaid him?

And after yanking him from the saddle, why had they carried him out here?

He thought about that as he walked over to his roan, and could find no logical explanation. It didn't make sense. Two men had ambushed him with a rope, had carried him for a few feet, and then dropped him like a sack of grain. Rimbaud fingered the bloody bruise on his head and swore morosely as he rode into the dark defile again.

Halfway through Rimbaud heard the roan's hoof strike metal, and guessed instantly that his gun lay in the dust. Dismounting, he felt for the Buntline and found it, and understood why he had been carried out of here. The two men hadn't been robbers. They had mistaken him for someone else, and toted him into the moonlight for a look at his face. He wondered who they had been after. Must be someone about his size and shape; someone they wanted to take alive. He was still thinking about it as he rode into Junction.

The town looked exactly as Rimbaud remembered it. Sprawled in the moonlight, its frame and adobe structures made an untidy pattern that began with a hodgepodge of stock pens here at the west end of Main Street and petered out near the base of Cemetery Hill to the east. He glimpsed the rose-tinted lights of Dulcy Fay's parlor house out at the end of Burro Alley where the trail crews camped. Dulcy, he recalled, was a big-bosomed, jovial woman who did her own shopping and bragged about the good table she set for her girls. According to town gossip, she had financed Sol Robillarde's successful campaign for the sheriff's office.

A piano in some home on Residential Avenue tinkled a lilting tune, and when Rimbaud passed the feed store's lamplit doorway a fat collie waddled out to bark at him.

"Ed Farnum's dog," Rimbaud said, and was surprised that he should remember so trivial a thing.

This, by God, was like coming home. At least it seemed like that for a man who had no more home than a jack rabbit.

Farther down Main Street two men stood talking on the plank walk that flanked Wells Fargo's wagon yard. Saddled horses and ranch rigs lined hitch racks in front of the Shiloh Saloon, Steinfeld's Mercantile, and the Alhambra Hotel. It occured to Rimbaud that this was Saturday. Recalling other Saturday nights spent in Junction, he smiled reflectively. There'd be a stud-poker game going at the Shiloh; might even be a dance at the Odd Fellows Hall. He had made no real friends here, strictly speaking, but he'd got to know a lot of people while he limped around waiting for his leg wound to heal. Remembering how he had ridden from the Ruidoso with a bullet in his thigh, Rimbaud smiled at the difference between that arrival and this one. He had been in bad shape for sure that night; so weak from loss of blood that he fell of his horse a mile from town and might have bled to death if a Good Samaritan hadn't toted him to Doc Featherstone.

Observing the lamplit windows of Eve Odegarde's restaurant just beyond Gabbert's Livery, Rimbaud felt a high sense of anticipation. He tried to remember if Eve's eyes were blue or gray, and was surprised that he couldn't recall their exact color. But he hadn't forgotten how those eyes could warm a man, deep down inside. Wide set, they were, with long black lashes that had made sooty shadows on her lamplit cheeks the night she

15

stood over there in the doorway and said good-by.

It occurred to Rimbaud now that Eve might have changed her ways a trifle in two years; might not be so strait-laced where men were concerned. Especially a man she hadn't seen in a long, long time. For Eve had liked him. She'd shown that plain enough. Rimbaud smiled. This might be more of a celebration than he'd planned on, if Eve happened to be in a receptive mood.

He was savoring the fine flavor of expectation when a man in the deep shadows of the stable doorway called sharply, "I got you covered!"

CHAPTER TWO

At nine o'clock Eve Odegarde blew out two bracket lamps in a room that had once been the parlor of a private residence but now held half a dozen oilcloth-covered tables. Because steamy warmth still flowed from the kitchen, where Limpy Smith was washing dishes, Eve left the street door open. There had been more customers than usual tonight, even for Saturday; folks from Spanish Strip and one family from way up in the San Marinos. More customers and more excitement. Then, just before closing time, Sheriff Sol Robillarde had ridden into town with three Roman Four riders, wanting to be fed.

Eve stopped in the doorway for a breath of fresh air, and recalled the talk she'd heard about Sam Maiben. According to Lew Stromberg, owner of the big Roman Four outfit, Maiben had been caught red-handed with a fresh-killed yearling that had a plainly botched brand. Eve sighed, wondering if posse riders still searching for Maiben would capture him tonight, and at this moment heard a man shout, "Roman Four! Roman Four!"

Stepping quickly out to the stoop, Eve saw a rider pulled up in front of Gabbert's Livery. His face was shadowed by a down-tilted hat brim but she thought at once: Sam Maiben!

Astonished that Sam should show himself in

17

town, Eve watched young Buck Aubrey ease from the stable doorway with a gun in his hand. She heard the Roman Four rider say, "You've butchered your last stole beef!"

Lew Stromberg and Ernie Link came running from the Shiloh Saloon. Other men came from Steinfeld's stoop and the hotel veranda; townsmen prompted by curiosity, and a few homesteaders from Spanish Strip—grim-eyed men like Al Shumway, Swede Severide, and Charley Bonn, who were friends of Sam Maiben.

Sheriff Robillarde hurried over from the courthouse. "No shooting, boys! No shooting!" he warned.

And now, as the tall rider nudged back the brim of his battered hat, Eve Odegarde stared at him in wide-eyed wonderment. The man sat high and lean-shaped in the saddle like Sam Maiben. He wore a black, flat-crowned Texas hat and rode a roan horse, like Sam. Even his moonlit face was familiar. But it wasn't Sam Maiben's face.

He had peered at Buck Aubrey in frowning silence for a long moment. Now he said, "Quit pointing that goddamn gun at me."

Eve recognized him then. "Jim!" she exclaimed, and saw Aubrey's mouth go loose-lipped with puzzlement. She heard him blurt, "You ain't Maiben!"

Lew Stromberg and Ernie Link came up to stand beside Aubrey. Stromberg peered at Rimbaud in narrow-eyed hostility, demanding, "Who are you?"

Rimbaud ignored the question. With his right hand close to his holster he said rankly, "Get out of my way."

There was a moment while resentment tightened Lew Stromberg's high-beaked face; while men out in the street stepped cautiously aside, 'leaving a wide lane beyond Rimbaud. The smell of trouble was that plain.

Eve watched Stromberg, fearful that he would draw. Lew Stromberg wasn't accustomed to taking orders. No man who knew him would be brash enough to give him one, for he was an uncrowned king in Quadrille Basin. She called urgently, "That's Jim Rimbaud," knowing what the name would mean to Stromberg and to every man who heard it. They might fail to recognize Rimbaud's whisker-shagged face here in the moonlight, but they wouldn't mistake the name that had become a gun-smoke legend on both sides of the border these past two years.

Lew Stromberg stepped aside, making room for Rimbaud to ride on into the barn doorway. "What you doing back here?" he asked.

"Minding my own business," Rimbaud said.

Eve watched him dismount, observing how gaunt and worn-out he looked; how much older and tougher and shabbier than when she'd last seen him. Like a border-jumping renegade, she thought, and heard him say to Joe Gabbert, "Give this horse a double ration of grain and all the hay he'll eat."

"Sure, sure," Gabbert agreed in the glib way of a free-talking man stirred up by excitement. "How's my old friend Francisco Durango?"

"Dead," Rimbaud muttered.

Lew Stromberg, who'd turned away, swung around instantly and demanded, "You sure about that?"

Rimbaud looked at Stromberg, remembering now that this man owned Roman Four, which had supplied Durango with free horses in return for range privileges across the line.

"You sure Durango is dead?" Stromberg repeated.

19

"Yes," Rimbaud said. "I was with him when he died."

For a moment no one moved or spoke. It was as if every man on this street was momentarily shocked to speechlessness. Rimbaud couldn't understand why the death of a rebel general should mean anything to them, one way or another. Durango had been liked in the border towns, especially by merchants and gun runners who welcomed his trade. But these men acted like they'd lost their best friend.

Lew Stromberg cursed and said, very distinctly, "The revolution is lost and so is my Mexican graze."

Jim Rimbaud could easily understand that part of it. Stromberg's reaction was that of an ambitious man who'd backed a loser he had hoped would win. But Rimbaud couldn't understand why all these others, townsmen and homesteaders, seemed equally disturbed by news of Durango's death. They had made no dicker for range with the rebels, and had no need to fear reprisal from victorious federal cavalry. Yet, as he strode through the crowd, Rimbaud heard a man announce apprehensively, "Now there'll be more trouble. Bad trouble."

Rimbaud nodded a wordless acknowledgment of Sheriff Robillarde's curt greeting and stopped in front of Eve Odegarde, inquiring, "Am I too late for supper?"

"Not if you'll eat in the kitchen," Eve said, showing him a composed and unsmiling face.

"Agreed," Rimbaud said.

Following her through the doorway, he wondered at her gravity. She had never been overly generous with her smiles, but he had expected one tonight. A man should rate that much welcome after being gone two years.

Eve turned and closed the door behind him and said, "You couldn't have brought worse news."

"What's so bad about it?" he asked, wholly puzzled.

Eve shrugged and said, "I'll explain it while you eat."

Then, as he took off his hat, she demanded, "Is that blood on your forehead?"

Rimbaud nodded and grinned at her, his eyes frankly appraising. She was, he decided, even lovelier than she had been two years ago; riper and more rounded, more womanly. Her hair, richly russet and drawn back to a braided bun at the nape of her neck, framed an oval face with high cheek bones. Her eyes, he saw now, were some warm shade between blue and gray, like campfire smoke. There was an expression like a smile in them now. Not a smile, exactly, for it didn't alter the composed fullness of her lips; more like a lingering reflection of something that had made her smile a long time ago. Something in the way she peered at him, as if a man's face were a printed page to be read and understood, prompted Rimbaud to bow, showing more graciousness at this moment than he had expressed in all the months he'd been away.

"Sweet Stuff," he said, using the nickname he'd given her in retaliation for being called "Fiddle-foot."

Eve smiled at that; a slow, reluctant smile that curved her lips. But she said censuringly, "You look awful, Jim. Purely awful."

"Worse than when I was here before?" Rimbaud asked with mock concern.

She nodded. "And ten years older."

Limpy Smith looked in from the kitchen, his bald head shining in the lamplight. "That ain't another customer, is it?" he asked complainingly.

"No," Eve said. "Just a shiftless saddle tramp

21

looking for a handout."

"Then I'll go," the old man said, and tromped back across the kitchen, his peg leg creaking at each step. When he went out the back door, Eve said, "Poor Limpy. He works all week to support a Saturday-night spree, and can scarcely wait to get it started."

Rimbaud followed her to the kitchen, recalling he had heard that Eve's father, once a respectable doctor, had died a drunkard. That was why she had turned this home into a restaurant.

"I'll fetch you a clean towel," Eve said, "soon as I stir up the fire a trifle."

Presently, as Rimbaud washed at the sink, she asked, "What brings you back to Junction, Fiddlefoot?"

"A woman," Rimbaud said, accomplishing a sly and secretive tone.

That seemed to startle Eve. Her eyes widened and for a moment she just stood there like a startled school girl. Looking at her now, Rimbaud had the profound conviction that she hadn't changed, and would not, where men were concerned. There wasn't a sprawly hair in her head, and oddly enough, he was glad that this was so.

"Do I know her?" Eve asked.

Rimbaud nodded. "She's just about your size and shape," he confided, reaching for the clean towel Eve handed him. "I came back to tell her the man had reformed."

"What man?"

"Fiddlefoot."

"Reformed how?" Eve asked, plainly skeptical.

"He's had his fill of fighting," Rimbaud said solemnly. "And of drifting, also. It took a little time for him to figure out there was nothing in it, but he finally got it through his thick noggin. And he learned it real good. You'd be surprised how he's changed, Sweet Stuff. It's downright astonishing. There was a time when he thought matrimony was a man-trap baited with home-cooked meals and the kiss-me look in women's eyes. But not any more. He might even decide to take out a homestead claim on Spanish Strip, or start a horse ranch in the San Marinos, or do some freighting for the Silver Bell mines. In fact, he's not particular, just so he had a home of his own and a sweet-loving wife to share it."

"How odd!" Eve exclaimed. "How very odd!"

"Sure is," Rimbaud agreed. "Beats anything that ever happened to me, man and boy, in twenty-eight years."

Eve was standing close to him, the woman scent of her hair making a perfume that roused a thrusting hunger in him. A hunger that had nothing to do with food. Prompted by an urge he couldn't resist, Rimbaud reached out and took her in his arms and said gustily, "Sweet Stuff."

"No, Jim!" she exclaimed.

"One kiss to welcome me back," Rimbaud urged.

Eve struggled to get free. She used her strength against him and commanded, "Let me go!"

Instead Rimbaud kissed her.

As if there were some potent magic in the merging, she ceased struggling at once. For a moment she was inert, neither rejecting his lips nor responding; her mouth loosely pliant and moist and sweet-flavored. Then she kissed him with a passionate pressing eagerness that astonished Jim Rimbaud and hugely pleased him.

It was like a wave, that kiss; a high-cresting wave warmly flowing over him and through him, possessing him completely. A wave that broke abruptly as she pulled her mouth away exclaiming, "Don't Jim—please don't!"

And at this moment, as he reluctantly released her, there was a knock at the front door.

Rimbaud watched Eve go into the dining room, her slim fingers hastily tucking up a lock of tumbled hair. He marveled at the monstrous difference one kiss could make. Five minutes ago Eve Odegarde had been a girl he had known briefly and admired. Now she was the woman he wanted to marry; the only woman he had ever wanted for a wife. By God, she had everything. Everything a man could want in a woman.

He grinned, thinking what it had taken to bring him here; how haphazardly Fate had intervened. The rebel defeat at San Sebastian, Durango's death, and his gold of liberation had fashioned the fabric of a renegade's return. Even the ambush back there on the stage road causing him to arrive after Eve's restaurant was closed, had been part of the fantastic pattern that had put her into his arms.

Rimbaud thought: My lucky day. The luckiest day of my whole life. And now, as he heard Eve speak to someone at the door, he jingled the seven double eagles in his pocket. The gold pieces wouldn't be squandered for a celebration at the Shiloh. A man bent on building himself a homestead cabin in the hills would need a few tools, a team of horses and a wagon. He would want a little money in his pocket when he braced Old Man Steinfeld for credit at the Mercantile.

Eve came back to the kitchen followed by a gaunt, gray-haired man whom she introduced as Charley Bonn. As they shook hands, she added, "You can do your talking at the table while Jim eats supper."

Bonn took a chair, his faded blue eyes intently appraising as Rimbaud went at the plate of warmed-up potatoes and roast beef Eve set before him. When she poured Bonn a cup of coffee the old man said, "Thank you kindly, ma'am," but he made no move to drink it. He just sat there whip-straight on the chair and fiddled nervously with his battered hat for a long moment before asking. "Was you planning to stay around here for a spell, Mr. Rimbaud?"

Rimbaud nodded, whereupon Bonn asked, "Would you take a ridin' job?"

"Starting your beef gather this early?" Rimbaud inquired.

Bonn shook his head. "It ain't that kind of riding," he said, and seemed embarrassed by the need for explanation. "It's—well, us fellers on Spanish Strip are having trouble with Roman Four. The beef market has been bad the last couple years and Stromberg held his steers off the market. Result is he's short of graze and spreading out in all directions. We figger he'll start crowding us worse'n ever now, on account of losing his Sonora range. He'll have to move his Mex herd north real quick or risk losing it to the Federals. Which means he's got to have more grass right away, or else sell a big bunch of beef steers for what they'll bring in an off market."

"So," Rimbaud mused, knowing now why the report of Durango's death had troubled the men on Main Street, and why Eve had said he couldn't have brought worse news. No matter which side won in a graze-grabbing fight, everybody lost something. Even the merchants. It seemed ironic that the collapse of an insurrection a hundred miles across the border should bring the threat of range war to Quadrille Basin.

"We saw how you made Lew Stromberg git out of your way," Bonn said, a plain note of admiration in his voice. "There ain't another man in Arizona Territory could make him move like that. Not one. It was a thing to see."

Rimbaud grinned and said, "Stromberg knew I'd beat his draw."

"Sure," Bonn agreed, "and now you've got the Injun sign on him, same as he's had on all of us, excepting for Sam Maiben. Stromberg never scairt Sam much, and we was depending on Sam to ramrod our fight agin Roman Four. But he had to hightail it."

He glanced at Eve, who sat near the back door, which she had opened. "Did you tell him how they framed Sam?" Bonn asked.

When she shook her head, he explained, "The law is after Sam. Swede Severide noticed a yearling steer with a brand that had been worked over from a Roman Four into a Boxed M, which is Sam Maiben's brand. From what Swede said, it was a botchy job and one you couldn't help from noticing, far as you could see it. Swede told Sam about it, figgering it was another of Stromberg's tricks to make us Spanish Strip folks look like a bunch of thieves. That's been Stromberg's way, all along, to accuse us of long-looping Roman Four calves and nagging at Sheriff Robillarde to arrest us on suspicion. Well, Sam rode out and shot the steer, intending to bury the hide so's there'd be no trumped-up evidence agin him. He was skinning it when Hugh Jubal, Roman Four's ramrod, and Sheriff Robillarde came riding towards him. There was nothing for Sam to do but run."

Rimbaud grinned. "So I got mistaken for a wanted cow thief," he said, and wondered why the name Maiben seemed familiar. Must be one of the men he'd played poker with at the Shiloh.

"Sam is no thief," Eve objected, very positive about this. "He's an honest, hard-working man who refuses to knuckle under for Lew Stromberg."

"It's just Lew's way of pushing Sam off his place and making it look legal," Charley Bonn explained.

26

"A man can't protect his property while he's in jail or dodging a posse, so Lew figures on gitting a wedge of Spanish Strip graze with a ready-made line camp to boot. I'd be willing to bet the price of a new pair of bench-made boots that Hugh Jubal worked that brand over, drove the steer to Maiben's range, and then went after Sheriff Robillarde. That's the kind of trick he'd be apt to play, being a man that's slicker'n cow slobbers when it comes to dirty work."

"Has Maiben left the country?" Rimbaud asked, not much interested.

"They'd of caught him if he hadn't, seems like," Bonn predicted.

But Eve said, "Sam wouldn't leave."

The old man glanced at her, and smiled, and said, "I guess not, considering. But he'll have to keep hisself hid. No Strip man would git a fair trial in this town. Not now, with Sol Robillarde slated for a seat in the territorial legislature and half the jury panel wanting to take his place as sheriff in the next election."

When Eve refilled Rimbaud's coffee cup he smiled contentedly, thinking how gracious a wife she would make. He contrived to press an arm against her aproned hip, and wished that Bonn weren't there to cramp their privacy. What more could a man ask than to be waited on by a woman like Eve Odegarde? Hell, he should've realized that two years ago. Recalling the passionate response of her lips, he said slyly, "The finest flavor I've ever tasted, bar none."

"Thank you, sir," Eve acknowledged, believing he referred to the coffee. But she didn't smile, and Rimbaud sensed a tension in her that puzzled him. It was caused by Bonn's talk of range war, he supposed, and wished the old coot would clear out. Eve should be sitting over here beside him now,

27

where he could smell the fine fragrance of her hair; close by him so that he could get an arm around her. They had a lot of honey-fussing to make up. Two years of it.

Presently Bonn said, "I'm beholden to Sam Maiben, same as some others. Our idea is to put a man on Sam's place who's capable of keeping Roman Four from taking over."

Rimbaud knew what he wanted then. And because there wasn't the remotest chance of his taking such a job, he said, "You'd have to pay high wages for a deal like that. Gun wages."

"Sure," Bonn agreed. "We figured on that. But it'd be worth what it cost, for we'd be doing ourselves a favor as well as Sam. Once Stromberg gits a toehold on Spanish Strip, it'd only be a matter of time until he'd start crowding the rest of us, and we'd have to fight for our rights."

"Sounds like the makings of a Sonora Serenade," Rimbaud said cynically. "That's what the newspapers called Durango's revolution."

"Will you take the job?" Bonn asked.

"Hell, no," Rimbaud said.

He thought that would end it; that his blunt rejection would convince Bonn so thoroughly that he'd leave him alone with Eve. There were things a man needed to tell the woman he was going to marry, and some of them should be said while she was in his arms.

Rimbaud went on eating for a moment. Then, observing how surprised and disappointed Bonn seemed to be, he said flatly, "I'm through siding underdogs. It's a losing proposition."

Charley Bonn sat there for a moment, absently tracing the steepled sweat stains on his hat band with a big-knuckled finger. Finally he said, "I calculated you'd be a man who'd pay a debt."

"What debt?" Rimbaud asked.

28

Bonn glanced at Eve, as if silently asking her intervention. But she merely shrugged, and now Rimbaud observed that she too seemed disappointed, which wholly puzzled him.

"What debt you talking about?" he demanded.

"You mean you don't know?" Bonn asked. "You ain't funning?"

Rimbaud shook his head.

"Well, according to what Doc Featherstone said two years ago, Sam Maiben saved your life."

"Saved my life?" Rimbaud echoed.

Then abruptly he understood, and the knowledge shocked him. He hadn't seen Maiben since that eventful night when the homesteader had picked him out of the road and toted him to town in a wagon.

"I'd forgotten what his name was," Rimbaud admitted. Aware of Bonn's intent gaze, he added, "It's my habit to pay a debt."

"Then you'll protect Sam's place?" Bonn asked eagerly.

Rimbaud nodded. He looked at Eve, and shrugged, and said, "So I take one more ride with the underdogs."

"Then Roman Four toughs won't be so brash when they hear you're at Boxed M," Bonn predicted smilingly. "They'll think twice before tangling with you."

But Rimbaud paid him no heed. He was looking at Eve's composed unsmiling face, wondering at her gravity and wanting to kiss the soberness from her lips. When Bonn had left, Rimbaud told her, "This deal will delay my plans a trifle, but they still stand, just like I said."

That seemed to embarrass Eve. A rich color stained her cheeks, giving them a peach-bloom loveliness in the lamplight. She asked, "Did you really mean it, Jim, about the homestead and all?"

"Sure I meant it," Rimbaud assured. "I meant every word of it."

"I didn't think you'd ever change," murmured Eve, as much to herself as to him. "I thought you'd go on being what you were as long as you lived."

She had been looking at him steadily, as if bemused by what she saw. Now she looked down at her hands, her smooth forehead faintly frowning. "I'm glad you've changed," she said, but she didn't appear glad at all. She seemed saddened by the knowledge.

Then she held up her left hand, and as Rimbaud peered at the small diamond ring, Eve said quietly, "I'm engaged to Sam Maiben."

For a moment, while the ironic significance of her words lanced through him, Rimbaud stared at the ring. It hadn't occurred to him that Eve might have accepted a suitor during the two years he'd been away. She had seemed so serenely self-sufficient, so independent and unresponsive to romantic advances, so resolute. He recalled now that she had refused Lew Stromberg's courtship, not because he was some twenty years older, but as she had put it, "Because I'd be marrying a ranch instead of a man." And now she was engaged to a homesteader wanted by the law. What a hell of a joke that was!

A self-mocking smile formed on Rimbaud's whisker-shagged face as he reached for his hat. "A shiftless saddle tramp thanks you for a fine supper," he acknowledged, remembering what she'd told Limpy Smith.

"Jim, I'm sorry," Eve said in a sincere, subdued voice that was scarcely above a whisper.

"That also is a losing proposition," Rimbaud told her, and went on into the dining room.

CHAPTER THREE

Ernie Link had been assigned the chore of watching the rear entrance to Eve Odegarde's restaurant. "Maiben will be getting hungry," Lew Stromberg had predicted. "He might just be fool enough to sneak in for a late supper."

It was a loco idea, to Ernie's way of thinking. A useless waste of time. A man might better be spending his leisure at the Shiloh bar, or with the girls at Dulcy Fay's parlor house. There was a new girl at Dulcy's who danced the can-can in her bare feet. A French Creole teaser from New Orleans. That's where a man should be on Saturday night, having himself some fun after pounding his rump asaddle all week. But there was no use trying to reason with Lew Stromberg. He was in a lather about losing that Mex graze in Sonora.

Standing in the shadow of Gabbert's wagon shed, Link watched the restaurant's lamplit doorway and caught a brief glimpse of Jim Rimbaud moving across the kitchen. Ernie grinned, recalling how spooked young Buck Aubrey had been when he found out who it was he'd mistaken for Sam Maiben. Buck wasn't much account with a gun, nor with his fists either, for that matter; and Rimbaud was supposed to be a heller from here to who hid the broom. Even Lew Stromberg wanted no part of him in a gun fight.

31

Link shaped up a cigarette and thought how it would be to have Rimbaud's reputation. A man like that could draw top wages anywhere, and have his pick of pretty girls. Folks listened to what he said, and got out of his way when he wanted to go someplace. With a rep like Rimbaud's you were a regular goddamn king. All you had to do was win a few fights. Instead of just talking tough, you had to act tough—be willing to tangle smack-dab, without a lot of windy warm-up. Like Rimbaud when he told Lew Stromberg to step aside. Lew had a terrible temper, and was fast with a gun. But the drifter's big reputation had made Lew act tame as a gutted calf.

A slight commotion in Gabbert's corral attracted Link's attention. Discarding the cigarette, he drew his gun and hurried around the wagon shed, thinking it might be Sam Maiben after a fresh horse. If he could just capture Maiben now, there'd be plenty of time to take on a few drinks and then go over to Dulcy Fay's.

But it wasn't Sam Maiben. It was just a back-eared bronc trying to hog the feed trough.

Ernie cursed, and on his return to the wagon shed observed Charley Bonn sitting at the kitchen table with Rimbaud. Mildly curious, Link eased across the moonlit alley and was standing close to the doorway when he heard Bonn ask, "Then you'll protect Sam's place?"

There was a brief silence before Rimbaud said, "So I take one more ride with the underdogs."

Ernie wasn't sure what that meant, until he heard Bonn say, "Them Roman Four toughs won't be so brash when they hear you're at Boxed M. They'll think twice before tangling with you!"

That was enough for Ernie Link. Going quickly to Main Street, he hurried toward the Shiloh Saloon. Lew would want to know about this.

Those Spanish Strip homesteaders might be hard to handle with a man like Rimbaud siding them. Perhaps Lew would want Rimbaud stopped right now; tonight. It occurred to Ernie that the man who killed Jim Rimbaud would make himself a rep in one fight. He would be known far and wide as being faster with a gun than Jim Rimbaud.

"He'd be famous," Link thought aloud. Then he skidded to a stop, barely missing a collision with Lew Stromberg's daughter, who came out of the Bon Ton Millinery with a huge hatbox in her arms.

She was a brunette beauty, this Della Stromberg. Just past nineteen, she seemed more like a big-city girl than the daughter of a Quadrille Basin cowman. She said smilingly, "You're just the man I'm looking for, Ernie," and pushed the hatbox into Link's hands. "Take it to my rig at the hotel while I pick up some yard goods at the Mercantile."

"But I'm in a big rush," Ernie objected. "Got somethin' real important to tell the boss."

Della laughed at him. "It can't be that important," she said, and left him standing there with the hatbox.

Link loosed a sighing curse. He was tempted to throw the goddamn hatbox at her—to tell the little bitch to tote her own bundles. But she'd get him fired. She had Lew eating out of her hand. Crossing Main Street's moonlit dust, he hoped no one would notice him. It wasn't fitting for a growed man to fetch and carry like a chore boy. You wouldn't catch Jim Rimbaud toting hatboxes for a tight-rumped tart. He'd tell her to go to hell, and slap her goddamn face if she got uppity with him. Lew's daughter had got too big for her britches since attending school in Tucson for three years. She acted like the Roman Four crew were her personal servants. And she had a way of using her eyes that made a man wonder.

33

Ernie thought: One of these days I'll catch her in the brush, and find out. Maybe that's what Della needed. Maybe it was what she wanted. You could never tell about girls like Della. They might be ripe as a juicy apple, just waiting to be plucked. But you couldn't tell until you tried.

When Ernie came to Della's red-wheeled buggy at the Alhambra hitch rack he observed Swede Severide and Al Shumway loafing in front of the hotel. He hoped they wouldn't notice what he was toting, but they peered at the huge hatbox and Swede said wonderingly, "Must be a new style Stetson built special for Roman Four heads."

Ernie cursed, and felt himself blushing like a schoolgirl waiting outside a locked privy.

"I bet it's real elegant," Shumway predicted. "The very latest fashion."

Severide chuckled. "Got a pink hat band, most likely, and a nice silky ribbon chin strap to keep it on when the wind blows. Wish I worked for a big outfit that paid such high wages I could buy stylish hats on payday."

Free of his burden, and burning with embarrassment, Ernie faced his tormentors. "You birds lookin' for a fight?" he demanded.

Al Shumway shook his head. But Swede, who'd had several beers since sundown, said, "There ain't no law against admirin' of a man's hat."

Someone on the hotel veranda laughed. That, and the grin on Swede's face, pressed the trigger of Link's temper. Striding toward Severide, he asked angrily, "What's so comical, Swede? What's so comical?"

"You," Severide said. His grin got broader and now, as he held both big fists cocked for fighting, he announced, "I've took too much from Stromberg bluffers who think they own the whole world. I'm thinkin' you're all gab and no guts, Ernie."

34

With a thrusting sense of tremendous outrage propelling him, Link drew his gun, lunged forward with it held head-high, and whipped it down. Severide attempted to dodge, but the barrel caught him across the left temple. He expelled a yeasty sigh and staggered sideways, colliding with Al Shumway, who tried to prop him up. But Swede went entirely limp, and Shumway, softly cursing, eased his friend to the plank walk.

"That'll learn him not to call me comical," Link muttered, backing slowly out into the street.

Swede's wife, trailed by two blond-haired youngsters, rushed down the hotel steps, and a man in front of the Mercantile called, "What's going on?"

Link holstered his gun. He stood in the middle of Main Street for a moment, not quite sure which way to turn. Then, seeing Jim Rimbaud go into the Shiloh Saloon, Ernie remembered the errand that Della Stromberg had interrupted.

"Damn her drawers," he muttered, and hurried toward the saloon.

CHAPTER FOUR

The moment Jim Rimbaud stepped through the Shiloh's batwing gates he understood that Lew Stromberg was waiting for him. The Roman Four boss stood with one elbow on the rosewood bar. He continued his conversation with Pat Finucane, the night-shift apron, and showed no slightest sign of interest. But he had been watching the doorway and now no longer watched it.

A negative, trivial thing, that withdrawal of attention. A thing most men would not have noticed. It was an involuntary observation on Rimbaud's part; a reflex sharpness of perception the smoky years had given him. For Jim Rimbaud wasn't interested in Stromberg as he walked to the bar. There was only one clear thought in his mind—the need for a drink.

"So ye finally came back," Pat Finucane greeted, resting his huge belly on the bar's beveled edge. He wore a derby all his waking hours to hide a head hairless as a doorknob; according to backstairs gossip, he even wore it while calling on Dulcy Fay, whose plump hand he had long sought in matrimony. "What'll ye have, Jimmy boy?"

"Bourbon," Rimbaud ordered, "and leave the bottle."

"Ah, so it's celebratin' you are. Or mournin' the death of that great patriot, Durango. Tell me,

36

James, how'd them North-of-Ireland Federals accomplish the killin' of Durango, God rest his weary soul?"

"A judas slut sold him out," Rimbaud said.

Finucane shook his head. "Wimmin," he muttered. "A man should have no dealin's with them whatsoever."

Then, as a man at the poker table called, "Bring us a bottle of Colonel's Monogram, Curly," Finucane added sighingly, "Nor with saloon clowns that think they're comical, bejasus."

Ignoring Stromberg, Rimbaud glanced at the poker table, where five men sat, their faces sharply etched in a cone of light from an overhead lamp. He identified Buck Aubrey, Joe Gabbert and Fonso Peal, who owned the saloon, and noticed that Limpy Smith stood propped against the side wall with an empty glass in his hand.

"Seat open for a poker player," Joe Gabbert called invitingly.

Rimbaud shook his head. He poured himself a brimming drink and downed it, and was pouring another when Lew Stromberg asked, "You in the market for a job?"

"No," Rimbaud said, not turning to look at Stromberg. And now, as he lifted his glass, Rimbaud glimpsed Ernie Link's reflection in the bar mirror. Link stood just outside the batwings and seemed to be signaling to Stromberg. Shifting his gaze to take in Stromberg's image in the glass, Rimbaud saw him nod; when he looked at the reflected batwings again, Link had disappeared.

"I pay top wages to top men," Stromberg said, as if there'd been no interruption. "I'm sending my West Camp crew across the line tomorrow to gather my Sonora stuff and could use a man like you to ramrod the job."

"Not interested," Rimbaud said.

Stromberg drained his glass, wiped his neatly trimmed mustache with the back of a hand, and suggested, "There might be a steady job for you with Roman Four—a good, high-paying job."

There was an edgy note of impatience in his voice that amused Jim Rimbaud. Stromberg wasn't big physically, but he possessed a thorough self-confidence and the established vanity of an ambitious man proud of his accomplishments. He was accustomed to having his way and resented rejection. It showed in his black eyes now as he said, "You could do worse than ride for me, Rimbaud. Much worse."

"Sure," Rimbaud agreed. "Which is what I'll be doing."

"What do you mean by that?"

Rimbaud shrugged and said quietly, "I'm riding for Sam Maiben."

Astonishment briefly changed Stromberg's face. "What for?" he demanded in a disbelieving voice. "Why would anyone ride for a posse-dodging thief like Sam Maiben?"

"The fun of it," Rimbaud said, not smiling. "Purely for the fun of it."

"You must be loco," Stromberg muttered, and seemed wholly baffled. "It doesn't make sense, Rimbaud. Not for a man like you. Why, he's nothing but a two-bit nester with a little jag of scrub cows a man could father between breakfast and supper, with time left to grease a wagon."

"It's a queer streak I inherited from a drinking grandfather on my mother's side," Rimbaud explained confidentially. "He was partial to bourbon whisky and underdogs."

Finucane, who was taking this all in, asked, "Was his name Moynihan?"

Rimbaud nodded.

"Black Bart Moynihan—the one they called the Boxer?"

38

"No," Rimbaud said. "His name was Tay."

"Must've been some shirttail relation," Finucane suggested, and peered wonderingly at Lew Stromberg, who strode angrily toward the doorway. "Now, what'd he stomp off like that for?"

Rimbaud chuckled. Observing his reflection in the bar mirror, he thought: I need a shave and a shearing. He wondered if the barbershop were still open. He had passed it on his way to the saloon but now had no recollection of seeing it. That realization filled him with self-contempt. A hell of a thing, him walking Main Street with his head so crammed with damn foolishness that he might as well have been blindfolded. It showed what happened to witless drifters who got romantic notions about warm-eyed women. They walked around in a perfumed fog.

Limpy Smith came up to the bar, his peg leg creaking. He peered at Rimbaud through booze-bleared eyes and said, "Seems like I've saw you before. But I can't recollect your name."

"Don't bother," Rimbaud suggested.

"Was you ever acquainted with Doc Odegarde?" Limpy asked.

Rimbaud shook his head.

"Well, Doc was a wonderful surgeon," Smith announced with a drunken man's insistence. "The best damned surgeon west of Chicago. You should have knowed him. I didn't think there was a white man in Arizona Territory that didn't know Doc Odegarde. Even sheepherders knowed him."

Rimbaud endeavored to ignore the dishwasher, but Limpy pointed to the knee-length stump of his right leg and bragged, "Doc Odegarde cut that off. If it hadn't been for Doc I'd of died deader'n hell four years ago. That's why I always tell folks about Doc Odegarde. A man who could do what he done shouldn't be forgot. If this town had any civic pride they'd put up a statue of Doc smack-dab in

39

front of the courthouse. It ain't fittin' for him to be forgot."

Pat Finucane waggled his bar rag at Smith and said, "Don't bother the customers, Limpy."

"Well, I'm a customer ain't I?" Smith demanded, drawing his scrawny frame erect.

Finucane spat behind the bar.

"Well, ain't I?" Limpy insisted.

"You," Finucane said sourly, "are a goddamn nuisance."

The drunken dishwasher wilted visibly. He looked, Rimbaud thought, like a lost dog nobody wanted; a homeless, lonely mongrel that folks booted off their back stoops. Limpy, he supposed, had attached himself to Doc Odegarde in the worshipful way of a stray dog wanting to belong to someone. But the medico was dead and Limpy was doomed to dismal aloneness.

Prompted by a kindred lack, Rimbaud said, "Hold up your glass, *amigo*, and I'll pour you a drink."

Smith gawked at him suspiciously, "You ain't funnin' with me?"

"Hell, no," Rimbaud assured him, enjoying the frown of disgust that rutted Finucane's cherubic face. "We'll drink a toast to your friend Doc Odegarde."

Limpy squinted at him, his toothless mouth sagged open with wonderment as Rimbaud filled his glass.

"We'll drink to Francisco Durango too, and all the brave ones who died at San Sebastian," Rimbaud announced. "By God, we'll have us a real celebration!"

They were on their third toast, standing with raised glasses, when Lew Stromberg came into the saloon. Had Rimbaud been watching he might have observed the brief, searching glance Lew sent toward a rear doorway. But Jim Rimbaud was saluting a departed comrade of the Sonora Serenade: "To Captain Rafael Hernandez, *insurrecto terrifico!*"

Lew Stromberg eased over to the poker table and was idly watching the play there when Ernie Link called sharply, "You lookin' for me, Rimbaud?"

He stood in the rear doorway of this long room, making an indistinct shape far back in the smoke-hazed shadows. Rimbaud peered at him, wondering who he was and what he wanted. Why should anyone think he was looking for them? Hell, he wasn't looking for anybody. Not even for a woman. Then, recalling what he'd seen in the bar mirror, Rimbaud understood that it was Ernie Link.

"Let's drink us another toast," Limpy Smith suggested.

"*Vamose,*" Rimbaud ordered, guessing what Link was up to. "Get away from me, friend—get away."

Smith couldn't comprehend the abrupt change in his drinking companion; the astonishing shift from chuckling cheerfulness to frowning gravity. Rimbaud had seemed so different, like he wanted to be sociable. But he was like all the rest, chasing a man off like he had smallpox. It was downright pitiful. "What hit you all of a sudden?" Limpy asked.

And at this same instant, as Rimbaud drew his gun, Ernie Link shouted in a shrill, high-pitched voice, "Step aside, Limpy! Step aside!"

But it was Rimbaud who moved. Wheeling away from the bar, he smashed the front bracket lamp with a shot that merged with the blast of Link's gun. That bullet whanged past Rimbaud's head to shatter a front window. Using the muzzle flare for a target, Rimbaud fired twice and stepped aside and heard Link yelp, "I'm hit!"

Rimbaud flicked a glance at Lew Stromberg, who stood in the bright island of light over by the poker table. The Roman Four boss was flattened against the wall with the others. He very plainly wanted to stay out of this fight.

Rimbaud probed the yonder shadows and waited, gun in hand. Even though Link was wounded, he might be playing possum, waiting for another try. The sneaky son had figured he would have all the best of it, standing back there and shooting at a lamplit target. But Limpy Smith had got in the way. That realization brought a cynical smile to Rimbaud's compressed lips. The drunken dishwasher was about the dorriest companion a man could have siding him in a fight, yet Smith had turned out to be his guardian angel here tonight.

Sheriff Sol Robillarde barged through the batwings, his heavy cheeks flushed with exertion. Bareheaded, freshly shaved, and wearing a white shirt minus its detachable collar, Robillarde looked more like a city politician than a sheriff. "What's all the shooting about?" he demanded.

"Go ask Ernie Link," Rimbaud suggested, and nodded toward the rear doorway. Holstering his gun, he turned to Limpy, who stood propped against the bar, and said, "Now we have another toast, *amigo*."

"Who to?" Limpy asked, straightening up.

Rimbaud grinned, not answering until he filled the glasses. Then, ignoring curious bystanders who had crowded into the saloon, he said gustily, "To Limpy Smith, the best one-legged man west of the Pecos!"

The pistol shots, heard throughout Junction,

had set off a welter of excitement. Rumors ran along Main Street like a flash flood, growing more fantastic with each repetition. A shirtless man leaned from a second-story hotel window and shouted, "They must've chased Sam Maiben right into town!"

Another man, hearing this as he ran down Residential Avenue, voiced the opinion that Maiben had been shot on Main Street. By the time these reports reached Dulcy Fay's place on Burro Alley they included the startling news that Sheriff Robillarde had chased Maiben into a vacant lot and was shooting it out with him, man to man.

"Good gracious!" Dulcy exclaimed, hugely pleased. "Sol will be a hero!"

The whole town was goggle-eyed with excitement. In the few moments it took Eve Odegarde to walk from her home to Steinfeld's Mercantile she heard announcements that Sam had been captured, that Swede Severide had shot Ernie Link, and that Jim Rimbaud was mixed in the shooting. Now, as she identified Della Stromberg in the sidewalk crowd, Eve asked, "What happened?"

Della gave her a brief glance and shrugged, thus expressing an inherent dislike for the woman her father had wanted to marry. But Charley Bonn's wife said, "Ernie Link came out Saloon Street with blood streaming from his right arm. Charley has gone over to find out what happened."

Eve went toward the hotel and presently, meeting Sheriff Robillarde, asked, "Who did the shooting?"

"Ernie Link and Jim Rimbaud," Robillarde said.

"Did Jim get hit too?" Eve asked.

"Not a scratch," Robillarde reported. "There's a bad one for any man to tangle with, that Rimbaud. The man is a born fighter, and has the luck of the Irish besides. Ernie should've known better. They

43

say he started it, and that he also pistol-whipped Swede Severide out here on the street. I've warned Lew Stromberg there's to be no more of that stuff, or Link will be locked up."

"And what did Mr. Roman Four say?" Eve asked with frank skepticism.

"Well, you know how Lew is," Robillarde said evasively. "He told me if I'd catch the Spanish Strip cow thieves that need arresting there'd be no room in jail for a Roman Four man."

"Do you think Sam Maiben is a thief?" Eve asked, and when Robillarde's eyes avoided her steady appraisal, she prompted, "Do you, Sol?"

"It's not a question of what I think, one way or the other," Robillarde explained with the practiced fluency of a born politician. "I have a warrant for Maiben's arrest, which will be executed to the best of my ability. After that it's up to a judge and jury."

Eve shrugged, understanding that Sol Robillarde would never allow anything to interfere with his ambition to become a member of the territorial legislature. A man needed the big cow outfits behind him to reach that exalted goal. And Sol Robillarde, who had once borrowed money from a parlor-house madam, intended to reach it.

The Sheriff walked on, speaking affably to others who asked questions. He was, Eve reflected, as gracious and seemingly honest as a man could be, but there were women in this town who resented his association with Dulcy Fay, and their opposition might defeat him at the coming election.

Eve stood there for a moment, watching traffic across on the Shiloh's lamplit stoop. Everyone in town seemed to have congregated on Main Street, the men investigating the saloon while their womenfolk waited, forming small groups along the sidewalk. A pair of riders trotted past whom Eve identified as Hugh Jubal and Red Shafter. She thought with a swift sense of relief: Two more Roman Four toughs who haven't found Sam!

She wondered where Sam was now, and if he was hungry. The poor man had been chased for hours. He might be laying out there in the brush somewhere wounded. Or dead. And whatever happened to him would be because of her. Lew Stromberg had made that plain enough the last time he'd called on her; he'd said, "You'll regret your foolish choice many times, and so will Maiben."

When Eve saw Charley Bonn come out of the Shiloh she maneuvered to meet him midway across the street. The old homesteader appeared worried. He said, "That shows what Stromberg will do to grab a piece of Strip graze. Link made it look like a personal grudge betwixt him and Rimbaud, but it was meant to be a chop-down, pure and simple."

"Is Jim still at the saloon?" Eve asked.

Bonn nodded. "I tried to talk him into leaving town with me, but Rimbaud said he had to help Limpy Smith finish off a quart of bourbon. Some darn foolishness about how important it was to drink twenty toasts."

"So Limpy has taken up with Jim," murmured Eve. And then she said something that didn't make sense to Charley Bonn: "Sam isn't a drinking man, thank God."

Bonn was wondering about that as he drove out of town with his wife. When he repeated Eve's words to Maria, she said, "The poor girl had a drunkard for a father, and is set on having a sober man for a husband. Anyone with a lick of sense would understand her feeling the way she does."

"But what's Rimbaud being drunk got to do with it?" Bonn asked.

45

"He could've been an old flame of Eve's for all we know," Maria suggested with feminine intuition. "Seems like I remember hearing Faith Shumway mention something about him sparkin' Eve Odegarde when he was here before."

"I wouldn't put no store in what Faith Shumway says, one way or the other," Charley muttered. "She's got a waggy tongue."

Presently, as Della Stromberg's rig went past in dust-swirling haste, Mrs. Bonn said, "You should've seen how she snubbed Eve right in front of folks tonight. It was downright brazen. You'd of thought Eve was some Burro Alley trollop the way Della treated her."

"Maybe it's the other way around," Charley said.

"What do you mean by that?"

"Nothing," Charley muttered. "Nothin' at all."

Women, he reflected, were always jumping to conclusions where scandal was concerned.

Which was approximately what Sheriff Robillarde was telling Dulcy Fay now as they stood in the shadows of Burro Alley. "You've got to understand how it is with me," Sol told her. "I'm running for a big office—an important office. And the churchwomen in this town are a bunch of jaw-wagging busybodies. They've already written to the governor complaining about me not arresting Roman Four riders who cause disturbances. They even hinted that I was on Stromberg's payroll, which is an outright lie."

Dulcy, who never spoke a word against anyone, said, "The poor souls have to do something to pass the time. Lord knows they lead humdrum lives, having religion and all."

Then she tugged at his sleeve and said, "Come around to the kitchen and have a cup of coffee, Sol. I'll put a slug of rum in it and we'll have a little party all by ourselves, like we used to."

"No," Robillarde said, "not tonight. And I wish you wouldn't come to my office, Dulcy. It'll just start talk again."

"You mean—you don't want to see me any more?" she asked, more surprised than angered.

"Not until after election," Robillarde said. "For God's sake, be sensible, honey. A man who's aiming for the territorial legislature can't keep company with a—well, with the proprietor of a parlor house."

Dulcy didn't speak for a long moment. She just stood there, her face an indistinct shadow in the darkness. Finally she said, "I offered to sell my place a year ago, Sol, so we could be married. But you told me not to. You said I'd be foolish to sell a good-paying business. I guess Pat Finucane is right. I guess all you wanted was that loan I gave you."

Whereupon she turned back along the alley. When she went into her house a bell tinkled and a customer in the parlor shouted, "There's the gal I want—the fat-fronted one!"

CHAPTER FIVE

Fonso Peal had replaced the smashed lamp above his bar and now helped serve a crowd of customers attracted by the fight. "It's an ill wind that doesn't blow some good," he confided to Finucane.

Pat mopped his perspiring face and grumbled, "It done me no good, bejasus, it's a percintage I should be workin' on this night."

Buck Aubrey came into the Shiloh and joined Lew Stromberg at the bar. "Ernie's right arm is broke," he reported. "Doc says it'll take upwards of an hour to fix a cast."

"Serves the wild hellion right for bustin' up a poker game just when I was winnin'," Joe Gabbert complained. "Whatever got into him, Lew?"

Stromberg shrugged, maintaining the attitude of a mildly interested observer. "Some personal grudge," he suggested.

Farther along the bar Jim Rimbaud stood listening to Limpy Smith's recital of Doc Odegarde's downfall.

"It was a woman that ruined the best surgeon Arizona ever had," Smith related. "She was his wife, and so shameful pretty it made a man catch his breath just to look at her. She had the finest head of sorrel hair you ever saw on a woman. Wore it high off her forehead in a pompadour that made her look like a queen. And she was built like a female women should be."

Limpy sighed and sipped his drink and said, "It sure beats all how a pretty woman can ruin a man, one way or another."

"Sure does," Rimbaud agreed, not quite drunk and not quite sober.

"I been ruined by several," Limpy admitted, "but they was the fancy, cat-eyed kind. Always differed if a man was goin' to hell on a blanket he might as well have some fun on the way. Which is why I did most of my triflin' with the sporty gals. I remember one in particular, at Tucson. There was somethin' about her that made a man itch, just bein' in the same room. A way she had of walkin', like there was dimples all over her. She took up with me right after I'd sold my half interest in a cow outfit. It took her two days and three nights to ruin me."

"How about Doc's wife?" Rimbaud prompted.

"Well, it happened one night while Doc was off attendin' some ranch woman that was havin' a baby," Smith explained. "He was the only medico in Quadrille Basin at that time, and his patients kept him busier than a boy killing snakes. I guess Doc spent more time takin' care of ailin' folks than he did at home."

Smith reached into a vest pocket for his Durham sack, that slight shift of position causing him to sway drunkenly. As if apologizing for unseemly behavior he said, "I can't hold my likker since the amputation. Doc claimed it was account of me havin' less room to absorb it."

"Shouldn't wonder," Rimbaud said. "What did Doc's wife do the night you mentioned?"

"Well, she got took by a bad attack of appendicitis and died deader'n hell. Doc was heartbroke. He went on a drunk right after the funeral and

49

never sobered up to the day he died. It was pitiful the way he mourned that woman. She was the ruination of him."

Limpy endeavored to sift tobacco into the paper, most of it missing. He gave up and put the sack back in his pocket, again swaying, and announced, "But Doc Odegarde was a crackerjack surgeon, regardless. Look how he carved this knee of mine."

As Rimbaud turned to look at the stump Smith raised for inspection, he saw Hugh Jubal and Red Shafter come through the batwings. Remembering that Jubal was Stromberg's foreman. Rimbaud thought: That makes five of them in town. He decided he'd had enough bourbon.

"Doc cut right through the joint," Limpy bragged, and lifted the leg so high he lost his balance.

Rimbaud attempted to grab him, but Limpy staggered sideways, colliding with Hugh Jubal, who swore irritably. Smith caught at Jubal's vest to right himself.

"Don't use me for no leanin' post!" Jubal protested.

He gave Smith a shove that sent him sprawling into the spittle-stained sawdust, whereupon Red Shafter cackled, "Behold the face on the barroom floor!"

Jim Rimbaud endeavored to convince himself that this was none of his affair; that Limpy Smith was just a drunken dishwasher who'd always be shoved around by someone. It was in the cards. But even as that reasoning ran through his mind, Rimbaud said sharply, "That's no fit way to treat a cripple."

"And who the hell are you?" Jubal demanded.

It occurred to Rimbaud that the Roman Four ramrod was like Lew Stromberg in the way he looked at a man. Like he was the main stud. The big casino. Jubal was a trifle taller and much heavier than his boss, but there was a similar arrogance in his eyes, the same intolerant tone to his voice. It was similarity that seemed rehearsed, and probably was.

Ignoring Jubal's question, Rimbaud helped Limpy up and heard Red Shafter say, "Why, that's the galoot you roped in Rimrock Pass this evenin'—the one we thought was Sam Maiben!"

Rimbaud brushed sawdust off Smith's shirt. The fall had dazed Limpy, for he asked, "What happened?"

"You got man-handled by a sneaking ambusher," Rimbaud said, loud enough for all to hear, and escorted Limpy to a chair at the deserted poker table.

There were eleven men at the bar, all watching this, and now Lew Stromberg said, "Hugh, that's Jim Rimbaud."

Jubal glanced around. "*The* Jim Rimbaud?"

Stromberg nodded. He motioned to Buck Aubrey, who followed him out to stand beside Jubal and Shafter. They were like that, four abreast, when Rimbaud turned away from the poker table.

A faintly derisive smile slanted Rimbaud's whisker-blackened cheeks as he observed the Roman Four line-up. It was an old established trick, he reflected; a traditional use of excess power to smother opposition. He had seen it in Lincoln County and on countless occasions across the border. Yet now, as he came on, Lew Stromberg said, "If my foreman waylaid you he made a mistake, and is willing to admit it."

Wholly surprised at this unexpected admission, Rimbaud peered at Stromberg and knew something that he hadn't even guessed before. But the puzzling implication of that knowledge baffled him. Despite all Stromberg's arrogance and all his vanity, the man was dominated by a calculating caution that seemed in direct contrast to his nature. Not cowardice, surely, or fear of physical harm, but a caution spawned by his greed for graze.

Rimbaud halted directly in front of Jubal and said, "I'm listening."

Hugh Jubal glanced at Stromberg, revealing in that brief gesture a slavish obedience. The thought came to Rimbaud that they'd fought the Civil War to free black slaves, yet here was a white man in bondage to his boss.

"Speak up," Stromberg commanded impatiently.

Hugh had no liking for this and showed it in the grudging way he said, "Well, it was a mistake."

"That's not enough," Rimbaud said.

An expectant hush settled on the room; a silence so strict that the ticking of a clock above the bar was a distinct disturbance. Anger brightened Jubal's brown eyes; it stained his frown-rutted brow and was a growling undertone when he muttered, "I'm sorry it happened."

"You should be," Rimbaud said. "Now tell Limpy Smith the same thing."

Jubal's eyes bugged wide with disbelief. "For just shovin' him off?" he demanded.

"For knocking him down."

Perspiration glistened against the sorrel stubble on Hugh's long upper lip and formed pimply beads across his forehead. Indecision gripped him so that he was like a man teetering on the top rail of a corral fence, and in this moment of suspension Fonso Peal said excitedly, "Smith was drunk and disorderly."

Without shifting his glance from Jubal's face, Rimbaud said, "You keep out of this, Peal." Then he asked, "How about it, Jubal? How about it?"

"Not by a damn sight!" Jubal shouted, emphasizing his refusal by shaking a first. "I ain't apologizin' to no drunken bum!"

He was like that, with one hand up, when Rimbaud tilted forward and hit him in the face.

Jubal's squalled curse was echoed by the meaty impact of another blow that mashed his nostrils. He floundered into Lew Stromberg and was still off balance when Rimbaud caught him with a sledging right to the ribs. Wholly confused by the swift savagery of Rimbaud's attack, Jubal skidded in a half turn, then reeled back like a drunken dancer doing an awkward sashay.

Men at the bar moved hastily aside, making room for him, and someone out front yelled gleefully, "Fight! Fight!"

Jubal braced himself against the bar. He wiped his bloody nose on an uphunched shoulder and peered at Rimbaud with eyes hate-polished to shining amber. "What the hell you tryin' to do?" he demanded in a wheezing, outraged voice. But he made no attempt to draw his gun.

"I'm teaching you some proper manners," Rimbaud said.

Downchinned and rashly smiling, he moved in with the relentless stalking glide of a hungry tiger. He had been sleepy and half drunk a few minutes ago; now the red rowels of physical combat roused a sharp clarity in him. And a familiar exuberance. This was how a man felt when he fought with his fists; when he used knuckles and muscles instead of bullets. This was the way a man was supposed to fight.

"Slug him, Hugh!" Red Shafter urged. "Swing at him!"

Jubal swung, and missed, and tried to duck away. But Rimbaud cuffed him back with lancing rights and lefts to the face. When Jubal grabbed him in a desperate attempt to clinch, Rimbaud flung him off, scoffing, "Don't use me for a leaning post."

Pat Finucane, who had come around the bar to assure himself of an unobstructed view, exclaimed amusedly, "Ain't he the droll one now, that Rimbaud!"

The mockery seemed to rejuvenate the battered Roman Four ramrod. Cursing insanely, he swung both fists and targeted Rimbaud with a glancing blow that peeled a strip of skin from Rimbaud's temple. He knocked Rimbaud back with a solid right to the chest, and when Rimbaud charged again, Jubal arched his body on the bar's beveled edge and kicked out viciously, trying for the groin. But Rimbaud crouched and caught the boot in both hands and hoisted it high.

Upended so violently that only his shoulders touched the bar, Jubal loosed a long-drawn yell as he went over, that frantic outcry merging with a crash of tumbled whisky glasses and the thudding impact of his body.

Rimbaud hurdled the bar, ignoring Fonso Peal, who protested, "You'll wreck my place!"

Jubal was up on one elbow, clawing for his gun, when Rimbaud slugged him. Hugh fell back and gave Rimbaud a blank, uncomprehending look and mumbled, "What the hell?"

Then his mouth sagged open and he was through.

Rimbaud grasped the back of Jubal's vest and dragged him slowly along the narrow runway. Rounding the bar's end, Rimbaud glanced at the poker table and observed that Limpy Smith was asleep with his head resting on the green felt. Something about that amused Rimbaud; he chuckled, thinking how odd it was that Smith should so serenely ignore the commotion he had caused.

Remotely aware of many faces at the doorway, Rimbaud dragged Jubal out into the soiled sawdust and dropped him face down. He wiped blood-smeared knuckles on his pants and looked at Lew Stromberg, who stood with a Roman Four man on each side of him, and asked, "Any objections?"

There was a ruddy flush on Stromberg's frown-creased face. His black eyes held a metallic shine and a queerly piercing intentness. It was as if he weren't quite sure what he was seeing, and must be sure before speaking.

"Any objections?" Rimbaud asked again.

"No," Stromberg said, his voice oddly mild and devoid of anger. "No objections."

Rimbaud grinned. He dropped a double eagle on the bar and said to Fonso Peal, "Set up drinks for the house."

Then he walked out, and stepping quickly through a crowd on the stoop, angled across Main Street toward the Alhambra Hotel. It didn't occur to him that Eve Odegarde might have been in that group of spellbound spectators, or that she would watch until he entered the hotel and then whisper, "Good luck, Fiddlefoot."

Promptly at midnight Pat Finucane hung up his apron, told Peal it was his quitting time regardless of customers, and made his customary pilgrimage to the big house in Burro Alley. It was characteristic of Finucane that he entered by the front door, for he was bewitched by his love for Dulcy Fay and cared not a damn that all Junction knew it. If he had asked her to wed him once he had asked her a hundred times.

Passing through the plush-carpeted parlor, he spoke pleasantly to a blonde girl whose garters were adorned by scarlet rosettes. She had smiled expectantly; now she shrugged at sight of his familiar Irish face and said, "So it's you again."

"Is Miss Dulcy out back?" Finucane inquired.

"And where would you expect her to be—in bed with Daniel Boone?" the girl asked irritably.

Pat paid her no mind. He hurried down the corridor to the kitchen and found Dulcy at the table with a coffee cup before her. "So here ye be, my cute colleen."

Dulcy smiled at him. She got up and poured another cup of coffee and took a fresh-baked pie off the window sill. "It's hot, and so's this kitchen," she said. "I've been that fidgety tonight I couldn't sit still."

" 'Tis a respectable home ye should be havin'," Pat said, eying her appraisingly and thinking that no other woman could look half so pretty with her sleeves rolled up and wearing a gingham apron. "This place will give you the runnin' fits if you stay in it much longer."

Dulcy sighed, neither accepting nor rejecting his prediction. She cut him a quarter wedge of pie and covered it with a slice of cheese.

"Ah, apple pie baked by the best cook east of west of El Paso," Finucane bragged, seating himself at the table. "A troublesome and tedious night it has been, what with shootin's and fist fights and customers galore. But at this moment I am the most fortunate of men, bejasus."

Watching the eager way he went at the pie, Dulcy smiled in wifely fashion. "You look," she said, "like a hardware drummer just off the Tucson stage. Let me take your hat, Finucane."

Pat grimaced. "I'd feel naked without it," he objected. "Bare naked."

"But do you sleep in it?" Dulcy asked, and when Pat shook his head, she announced, "Then it's merely a matter of time until I'll see you naked, Finucane."

"How so?" Pat demanded.

Dulcy laughed at him. "Do you suppose the preacher would marry us with you wearing a hat?"

Finucane peered at her, a slow, wishful smile on his cherubic face. "Do ye mean we're to wed?" he asked. "Have ye seen through that spalpeen Robillarde at last?"

She nodded, whereupon Pat cried, "Dulcy—Dulcy darlin'!"

And then he did an odd thing. He took off his derby.

CHAPTER SIX

The hot glare of noon's shadowless sunlight was on Main Street when Jim Rimbaud came out of the Alhambra Hotel. He had slept the clock around, yet he didn't feel rested. He had downed two cups of black coffee in the dining room but still felt sluggish and depressed. Even the cigarette he smoked didn't taste right.

"Too much bourbon last night," Rimbaud reflected moodily.

But he knew it was more than that. This wasn't an ordinary hangover caused by indulgence after long abstinence. It was spawned by a bleak sense of futility and frustration. He had come to Junction with the most peaceful intentions a man could have, wanting food and rest and another look at Eve Odegarde. But he had been challenged at every turn. Resolved to quit the gun game, he had been obliged to take on the sorriest chore in the book—protection of a homestead against big-outfit invasion. And Eve Odegarde was engaged to the man he was obligated to. It seemed as if the whole damned deck was stacked against him.

Rimbaud cursed. He discarded the cigarette and gave Main Street a squint-eyed appraisal. The town had looked good to him when he rode in last night. A moonlit oasis. A sanctuary where a trail-spent traveler could rest his weary bones. But now Junction's warped planks and dilapidated buildings stood revealed in all their harsh reality. A saddled horse stood slack-hipped at the Shanghai Café hitch rack, its hind feet fetlock-deep in manure. Diagonally across the street a sour-faced old man swamped off the Shiloh stoop with a bucket, and shook his mop at a dog hunting shade in the saloon. The cringing mongrel reminded Rimbaud of Limpy Smith. He wondered how the dishwasher felt today, and if he remembered his drinking companion of last night.

Probably not, Rimbaud thought. But he would remember Limpy Smith as long as he lived, and cherish the memory. It was one bright spot in all this sorry mess.

When the old swamper plodded into the saloon the street was deserted. But presently, as Rimbaud passed an intersection, he observed people coming out of a church on residential Avenue. Remembering that Eve Odegarde closed her restaurant on Sundays, Rimbaud wondered if she was in that group, and was tempted to loiter here on the chance of seeing her. Then he shrugged and went along toward Gabbert's Livery. No sense tantalizing himself with the sight of a woman who belonged to someone else. Better to forget all about her. There were other women in the world. A hell-smear of them. Ripe, warm-eyed women that a man could have for the taking.

Sheriff Sol Robillarde came out of the Shanghai Café and stood there prying at his teeth with a toothpick while Rimbaud walked up to him. "Good morning," Robillarde greeted in a blandly impersonal voice. "What's this I hear about you riding for Sam Maiben?"

"You heard right," Rimbaud said.

"But the man is a fugitive from justice," Robillarde insisted. "A wanted cow thief. Why get mixed up with him?"

"My business," Rimbaud said.

59

"You're just asking for trouble," the Sheriff warned. "No matter what some folks may say about Lew Stromberg, he has done nothing illegal and his crew has been deputized as a posse to capture Sam Maiben. I want to be fair with you, Rimbaud. I want to say here and now that what happened last night was no fault of yours. But I'm warning you that any interference with the capture of Maiben will not be tolerated."

Rimbaud laughed at him. He asked, "Would that be a threat or a warning, Sol?"

"A warning. My political future may depend on what takes place in the next few days. I want no more trouble for the newspapers to puff up into headlines. Don't want it, and won't stand for it."

"So?" Rimbaud mused. "Well, now I'll tell you something, Sol. Any Roman Four rider that trespasses on Maiben's property will do so at his own risk. And to hell with your political future."

Robillarde shook his head, plainly displeased yet showing no anger. He was, Rimbaud thought, a thoroughly patient man with a single purpose in his mind.

"You're just asking for trouble," Robillarde warned again. "Just asking for it."

"Sure," Rimbaud peered, "Like I asked Ernie Link to take a pot shot at me from the Shiloh's back door."

Then he went on to the stable to have his horse saddled. Joe Gabbert came out of the harness room, tousle-haired and yawning. "A big night," the liveryman reflected. "You leavin' so soon?"

Rimbaud nodded, handed him a silver dollar, and asked, "Which is the best way to Sam Maiben's place?"

"So them rumors is true," Gabbert said. "Well, Sam couldn't have a better man sidin' him, by grab. You got Lew Stromberg eatin' out of your

60

hand. Never saw the beat of it, the way you bluffed Lew down last night."

"I wasn't bluffing," Rimbaud said. "How about some directions?"

"Well, the Spanish Strip road forks off to the north a mile beyond the cattle pens. Just keep on it till you top Big Mesa, then bear left on a trail that drops off into Embrace Canyon, cross the creek, and climb Jigsaw Divide. You can see the whole damn world from there, includin' Roman Four which lays due west quite a piece, and Maiben's place off to the north about five crow-flight miles from Big Mesa and branches off at Isabelle's Camp. But it's a good piece farther that way."

"Thanks," Rimbaud said and rode out.

"You sure gave Hugh Jubal one hell of a trouncin' last night," Gabbert called, following him to the sidewalk. "That's one time Hugh really got upset." He laughed at his joke and asked, "Ain't that a dilly?"

But Jim Rimbaud didn't hear it. He was watching Eve Odegarde go up her front steps; was seeing how lovely she looked in a fashionable dress and a plumed pancake hat that tilted coquettishly atop high-coiled russet hair. That, he supposed, was how her mother had looked. Like a queen.

Eve was opening the door when she saw him. One gloved hand came up in a little gesture of surprise and for an instant she seemed on the verge of calling out to him. But instead she went inside and closed the door.

Rimbaud wondered about that as he rode out of town. Why hadn't she spoken to him? Didn't she consider it fitting to associate with drifters on Sunday?

"To hell with her," Rimbaud muttered and spat into the dust. There was no damn use trying to figure what went on in a woman's head. They were wholly unpredictable. But he couldn't help remembering how it had been with her in his arms last night. For that brief interval, while she gave him the wild sweet flavor of her lips, Eve Odegarde had been his woman.

Rimbaud grinned, recalling how surprised and pleased he had been; and how abruptly she ended the kiss. Eve, he guessed, was equally surprised by her passionate response. And perhaps a trifle ashamed. It was as if he had aroused an elemental urge that she had hitherto reserved for the man of her choice—meant only for Sam Maiben. And she had been shocked that a fiddlefooted drifter should have caused her to reveal it.

Perhaps that was why she hadn't spoken to him, Rimbaud guessed. She was ashamed of herself, and angry at him. He was past the cattle pens when he noticed a smoke-like plume of dust rising above brush far ahead. One rider, he judged, and gave the long slope a continuing attention, observing its gentle rise to a rock-crowned ridge that ran north and south.

The Roman Four crew would be on the hunt for Maiben again today, he supposed. At least the headquarters crew, which, according to Limpy Smith, consisted of five men. Two others, who held down a line camp in the Potholes, probably hadn't been in on yesterday's man hunt. But there was another Roman Four man unaccounted for in town last night—a fellow Limpy called Booger Bill. "Big as a Percheron stud," Smith had described him, "and a trifle loco in the noggin."

Even with Ernie Link out of it, and the West Camp crew gone to Sonora, there'd be at least five men riding today. And judging by what had happened in town last night, they wouldn't be particular which target they shot at—Sam Maiben or his hired man. That realization brought a sardonic smile to Rimbaud's face. This would be the Ruidoso all over again. Another Sonora Serenade: On a smaller scale, of course, but with the same gun music, the same bloodstains in the dust.

"I'm a goddamn chump," Rimbaud told himself. "A silly, woman-wanting chump."

The smoky years had taught Jim Rimbaud the value of vigilance on the trail so that now, observing that the distant dust plume had vanished, he angled off the road. The unseen rider, he decided, had halted somewhere south of the road on a brush-blotched ridge that bulged the long slope. His presence up there might not mean a thing. But from now on, day or night, the threat of ambush would be a nagging companion, and wariness would be his only shield.

He crossed the slope some three miles north of the ridge, and presently re-entering the Spanish Strip road, followed it to the broad crest of Big Mesa. Here he halted, scanning his backtrail and giving the roundabout terrain a questing attention. No risen dust showed anywhere and no sound disturbed the windless, sun-warmed air. When he turned into a westward trail he noticed two sets of horse tracks—one set headed toward the road, and another set angling away from it. Keeping to one side of the tracks, he observed a similarity in the hoofprints, as if they might have been made by the same horse. But the tracks were five or six hours old, he judged, and so disregarded them as his horse eased down a narrow, steep-tilted trail into Embrace Canyon.

Presently, as the roan drank from a pool in a boulder-strewn creek at the canyon's bottom, Rimbaud had an overwhelming urge to take a swim. This was more water than he had seen in months. Not enough to swim in, really; but a man

63

could splash around in it and get himself wet all over.

Rimbaud scanned the towering wall of Jigsaw Divide, which rose high above the canyon. This might be one of the places Roman Four would watch in the hunt for Sam Maiben. But he detected no sign or sound of movement anywhere on the divide, and the water was hugely tempting.

"I'll risk it," Rimbaud decided with a gambler's fatalism.

Tying the roan to a clump of brush, he took off his clothes and eased into the pool. This was better than any barbershop bathtub. It reminded him of his boyhood in Texas; how he used to ride ten dusty heat-hammered miles for the boyish pleasure of taking belly-splashers in a muddy river. There had been no other boys to share the fun, but he had whooped and hollered, making believe that he was accompanied by rollicking companions. He recalled the fine feeling of the water against his flesh when he first jumped in, and how his father had poked fun at him, warning that he'd grow up web-footed. A long, long time ago. . . .

Rimbaud was splashing around and thoroughly enjoying himself when a voice called, "Is that you, Sam?"

A woman's voice.

Jim Rimbaud crouched motionless for a moment of bewildered disbelief. What would a woman be doing here? And couldn't she see that he was naked as a newborn babe?

He turned his head and saw her standing in a cleft of rock above the creek. Her smiling face, beneath the upcuffed brim of a gray hat, was not familiar to him, and now an expression of astonishment swiftly altered it.

"Why, you're not Sam Maiben!" she exclaimed.

"No, ma'am," he said, and waited impatiently

64

for her to leave. But she remained there, peering down at him with a frank curiosity that embarrassed him. Why didn't she go on about her business?

Angry now, Rimbaud retreated from the pool, keeping his backside to her. He slipped on a wet rock, teetered momentarily with flailing arms, and fell in splashing confusion. It was hugely embarrassing, for he landed all spraddled out, and when he looked up, there she was, still watching him. Some homesteader's bratty daughter, he supposed, gawking at the first man she'd ever seen in the raw. Well, by God, she had got a good look. She had seen everything there was to see. A girl like that deserved a good kick in the pants.

He didn't look at her again as he strode out of the creek, making no attempt to conceal his nakedness. But he had the feeling that she was laughing at him. He had his pants on and was using his shirt to dry his feet when she came down, leading a saddled horse.

"You must be the Jim Rimbaud they're talking about," she said, smiling. "I missed seeing you in town last night."

Rimbaud ignored her. He pulled on his boots, shook out his damp shirt, and shrugged into it with the casual ease of a man dressing in the privacy of his own home. But he was seething with resentment, knowing how comical he must have looked falling on his rump out there in the creek. He wondered who she was; and why, mistaking him for Sam Maiben, she had seemed so pleased at finding him naked in knee-deep water.

"So you're the one who shot Ernie Link and gave Hugh Jubal a beating," she said with seeming satisfaction.

Rimbaud nodded, now convinced that she was a Spanish Strip homesteader's daughter. He met her bold inspection with an appraisal equally deliberate, seeing that she had brown eyes and black hair and pouty, full-lipped mouth. There was a dust smudge on her nose, and tiny beads of perspiration on her temples. Young, he thought; not more than nineteen or twenty. She wore denim riding pants that revealed shapely thighs, and a man's cotton shirt that seemed a trifle too large except across the twin swell of her high breasts.

"Who are you?" he asked.

"Della Stromberg."

"Not Lew Stromberg's daughter?" Rimbaud demanded in disbelief, and when she nodded, he still couldn't believe it.

"Surprised, aren't you?" she said. Then her lips curved into a faintly cynical smile and she explained, "Roman Four comes first with my father, but not with me. There's more to living than grass and water and the size of a calf crop. I ride where I please and make friends where I please."

"Is Sam Maiben a friend of yours?" Rimbaud asked.

"A very good friend," she said smilingly.

Jim Rimbaud stared at her. What the hell was this? The daughter of Lew Stromberg professing friendship for a man who stood acussed of stealing from her father. It didn't make sense. Nor could he understand why she should be looking at him in such intimate fashion right now. Hell, she knew he'd shot one of her father's men and fist-whipped his ramrod. Yet she was smiling at him. There was something wantonly female in her eyes; a teasing look that seemed like invitation, and a sense of receptiveness that aroused a man. He had known brazen women who were boldly pliable to the ways of men, but they hadn't been daughters of proud and prosperous cattle kings.

"What kind of a brat are you?" Rimbaud asked

with the blunt honesty of a man wholly puzzled.

"Don't you call me a brat!" she objected.

Rimbaud watched anger stain her cheeks. It was an odd thing. She had seemed so completely self-contained a moment ago, but now she was all fire and passion. Even her lips seemed redder and fuller. She reminded him of the hot-eyed dancer who had betrayed Durango. There was the same sulky look to her now, as if she would bite in the clinches.

Rimbaud grinned at her and said, "A brat if ever I saw one."

"Why you—you dirty trail tramp!" she raged.

And then she slapped him.

Rimbaud reached out and grasped her by both arms. Her hat fell back to hang by its throat thong and her hair came down in disorder. Struggling to pull free, she was like a panting dancer, and the musky woman smell of her was a pungent perfume. There was nothing self-contained about her now. Squirming and twisting, eyes flashing, she was the living image of Durango's Sonora woman doing her dance in a candlelit cantina.

"Pretty," Rimbaud said. "Pretty enough to kiss."

"Take your hands off me!" Della insisted, her voice shrill with outrage.

Rimbaud pulled her in, and missing her mouth, drew his lips across her cheek.

"Don't you dare!" she panted.

The shirt she wore had been open part way down; now as a button popped, one of her breasts was fully exposed. That hugely pleased Jim Rimbaud. He said, "Now you know how it feels to be gawked at," and eyed the rosette-like nipple with exaggerated delight.

"You beast!" she cried. "You awful beast!"

Rimbaud laughed, and used his shoulder to force

her face around. When she bit his ear he loosed a gusty chuckle, saying, "Just like Sonora."

Then he found her lips.

It wasn't much of a kiss, for she continued to struggle. Rimbaud released her, and stepped back and watched her hastily fasten the top buttons of her shirt. He said, "I called you a brat for staring at me in the pool."

Her face was flushed and she was still breathing hard. "Do you make it a habit to kiss brats?" she asked scornfully.

"Only when they slap me," Rimbaud said. He took out his Durham sack and absently shaped a cigarette while watching her rearrange her tumbled hair. "Were you looking for Maiben when you found me?" he inquired.

Della nodded. "I wanted to warn him that the headquarters crew is strung out between his place and Charley Bonn's. They figure he'll make a try for supper tonight. I brought him some sandwiches."

"So," Rimbaud mused, thinking about the engagement ring on Eve Odegarde's finger, and what this girl could do to a man forced to hide out in the brush. She was a teaser if ever he'd seen one. She had backed away from him, keeping a safe distance, and seemed on the verge of flight. "Does your father know you associate with Maiben?" he asked.

"No, and he'd be furious if he found out. Which he will, of course, sooner or later. But I—well, I like Sam a lot," she admitted, very frank about this. Then she added, "Sam is a born rebel, and so am I."

Rimbaud grinned, and quoted a line from a poem that had been a Texas schoolboy's favorite: "Rebels ride proudly in the sun."

"Counting the victory already won," Della said, all her anger fading.

68

It was like a bridge between them, that poem they both liked. A mutual strand of fellowship that made it seem quite natural for her to accompany him on the ride up the west wall of the canyon. When they rested their horses on a switchback turn, Rimbaud looked down and said, "I wonder where it got the name Embrace."

"There's a nice story attached to that," Della reported. "It goes back to the time when this was part of Mexico. Want to hear it?"

Rimbaud nodded, whereupon she told the ancient legend of Embrace Canyon—how a highborn daughter of a rich Spanish cattleman fell in love with an American outlaw called the Calico Kid. Chased by *rurales*, the Kid took refuge in a cave near the canyon's rim and was supplied with provisions by the girl, Rosita.

"They were madly in love," Della explained, "and Rosita came here whenever she got the chance. Can't you just picture those two, keeping their love trysts here? For all we know they may have stood on this very spot, or bathed together down there at the pool. It must have been truly beautiful, especially on moonlight nights. There's something so romantic about the canyon."

"Must be," Rimbaud reflected, slyly smiling at her.

Della flushed, and instinctively fingered the buttons of her shirt to be sure they were fastened. Then she continued with the story. "One day, just at sundown, the *rurales* closed in on them. Knowing there was no escape, the Calico Kid kissed his sweetheard farewell and told her he was going to jump off the rim of the canyon, preferring death here where they'd been so happy to life in prison without her. But Rosita clung to him, saying she couldn't live without him, for he was part of her. The important part. I think she was right. I think real love is like that, don't you?"

"Could be," Rimbaud said, understanding how romantic a daughter Lew Stromberg had sired, and marveling at the knowledge.

"I suppose the Calico Kid tried to talk her out of it, manlike," Della continued. "But Rosita clung to him, and as they jumped together, disappearing into the canyon's blue shadows, the *rurales* heard their voices merged in a kind of singing laughter that echoed back and forth across the canyon. Next morning their bodies were found locked in a lovers' embrace, and that's how the canyon got it's name."

"An odd story to fit an odd name," Rimbaud mused.

"There's a saying that each year on the anniversary of their death the singing laughter can be heard by all who've ever lost a lover," Della said, and smilingly inquired, "Are you eligible to hear it?"

Rimbaud chuckled. "In a way, perhaps," he admitted, thinking of Eve Odegarde.

As they rode on up the trail, he asked, "Is the cave nearby?"

"We'll pass it just before we rim out at the top," Della said.

The trail was steep here, twisting a tortuous way between jutting bastians of upthrust rock. The horses clawed for footing on tilted slab formations that radiated afternoon's sharp sunlight, bringing out sweat. Once, when Della raised an arm to wipe her flushed face, Rimbaud observed how perspiration had stained the armpit of her shirt. And he wondered why that sight roused more throbbing passion in him than had the exposure of her breast.

"Hot, isn't it?" she said. "But there'll be a breeze at the top. There always is."

She was a queer one, Rimbaud reflected. Her voice and manner of speaking gave the impression of a gracious, well-educated girl. Yet she reminded him of the *solderas*—those bold-eyed women who had followed Durango's ragged rebels from camp to camp, sharing their sorry blankets. She had the same shrugging disregard for risk or hardship; the same appearance of pagan resiliency. He wondered if she would accompany him to Maiben's cabin. And guessing that she might, he felt a rising sense of expectancy. Guarding an abandoned homestead wouldn't be so grim a chore with a girl to keep him company. He grinned, thinking how mixed-up a deal this might become.

Nearing the top now, Rimbaud kept his eyes sharply focused on the rimrock ahead. Della's report that the Roman Four posse was concentrated somewhere beyond Maiben's place didn't mean a thing. There was no telling where inquisitive man-hunters would prowl. There might be one waiting up there now, wanting a target he wouldn't miss. Rimbaud was steadily watching the sky-lined crest when Della said, "There's Calico Cave, off to your left."

And at this same instand, as Rimbaud turned to look, she exclaimed, "Sam!"

CHAPTER SEVEN

Sam Maiben made a tall, lean shape standing there in front of the cave with a grin creasing his darkly stubbled cheeks. He wore a battered black hat nudged back so that an unruly lock of brown hair slanted across his forehead. There was a long rip in the right sleeve of his faded blue shirt and bachelor patches at both knees of his soiled riding pants. But it was his bloodshot eyes that marked him most plainly, giving him the look of a renegade on the run. Even now, as he smilingly greeted Della, those eyes retained a shifting uneasiness.

Remembering how frequently he had been mistaken for this man, Rimbaud thought: So that's how I look. He was not pleased by the knowledge.

"I've brought you something to eat," Della announced, going to Maiben at once.

"Good girl," Sam praised, but his chief attention was for Rimbaud. He came out to the trail and offered his hand and said, "I met Charley Bonn over on Big Mesa last night. He told me you had agreed to guard my place. I'm sure much obliged for your help."

Rimbaud shook hands, taking a leisurely look at the man who had won Eve Odegarde's affections. "Just a case of paying off a debt," he said, and reckoned Maiben's age at twenty-four to -five.

"Charley told me that you gave a couple of Roman Four toughs their needings," Maiben said smilingly. "I would have liked to see that, especially the fight with Hugh Jubal. He's the dirtiest dog in Quadrille Basin."

Della asked, "Did you have any narrow escapes, Sam?"

"Half a dozen," Maiben said, and grimaced. "They almost pocketed me in the roughs south of Canteen Creek, and again when I tried to sneak into Swede Severide's place. Booger Bill stayed at my heels half the night."

Maiben hadn't slept and showed it in the strained, bloodshot condition of his eyes and in the nervous way he kept glancing up the trail. He said. "I dislike to shoot a man, but I'll put a bullet in that Booger Bill if he pesters me tonight."

"Serve him right," Della agreed.

Observing the way she looked at Maiben, Rimbaud was mildly amused. Della couldn't keep her eyes off him, or her hands either, for now she brushed dust from his shirt sleeve. Her eyes held the look of a squaw waiting to serve her brave.

"I won't need to worry about my place, with you there," Maiben said. "I'm sure pleasured to have you siding me."

Rimbaud shrugged and said frankly, "I had no choice, considering."

Then Della asked poutingly, "Aren't you glad to see me too, Sam?"

"Sure," Maiben said. "Sure I am. Especially if you brought something to eat. I'm hungrier than six Sonora Steers."

Della turned quickly to the saddlebags on her horse, bragging, "I've got beef sandwiches, ground coffee, a canteen of water, and a coffeepot. Also three airtights and some sack tobacco."

"*Bueno!*" Maiben exclaimed. He grinned up at Rimbaud and said, "Light down, Jim. We'll have us a picnic."

Rimbaud glanced at Della, who was busily unloading the saddlebags. She didn't speak, and so he said, "Reckon I'd better ease on over to your place and take a look around before dark."

Presently, when Maiben had made certain suggestions, Rimbaud rode up the trail. It seemed significant that it was Sam, not Della, who had invited him to remain. She hadn't wanted a third person at the picnic; she'd shown that by her silence, and by the sprawly look in her eyes. But Maiben had seemed more interested in the food than in the girl who fetched it.

There was a breeze at the crest, as Della had predicted. Except for a few wind-warped piñon, the divide's high-arched back was bare of vegetation. Halting on its topmost shelf of slab rock, Rimbaud gave the surrounding country a questing attention. Westward, beyond a series of secondary ridges and the valleys between them, lay a vast region of long flat-topped mesas. In the far distance, where a road ran string-straight across a heat-shimmering plain, he detected the remote flash of a windmill's revolving blades. That, he supposed, would be Roman Four headquarters, and calculated the distance as being upwards of a dozen horseback miles. Perhaps farther. Northward the land fell away in broken ranks of timber-hung hills that leveled off into a broad strip of benchland. A sun-silvered ribbon of water made a serpentine shine where it looped across a distant meadow turned tawny by summer's heat.

"Good country," Rimbaud mused with a cowman's eye for graze. Then he added cynically, "Too goddamn good."

For that was the unchanging history of cattleland. Good graze had invariably spawned trouble ever since the Israelites ran their herds on the hills east of Jerusalem. There had been greedy men then, wanting to spread out and willing to fight for that privilege. Times had changed, but human nature hadn't. Greed and lust still ruled the roost. Men grabbed for gold or graze or women as they'd always grabbed. And the strong still trampled on the weak.

"Dog eat dog," Rimbaud muttered, and focused his sun-squinted eyes to a search for Maiben's place. He glimpsed a windmill above the brush to the northwest, and presently, riding down a deep-grooved trail, caught a metallic glint a trifle to the south. It seemed to come from a low ridge, disappearing and returning, as if a piece of moving metal were reflecting sunlight.

Rimbaud gave the ridge a concentrated attention for fully five minutes, detecting no sign of movement save the occasional flash. There seemed to be only one logical explanation: A hobbled horse with a silver-mounted bit would make a flash as it browsed on brush or fought flies.

So Stromberg has sent me a visitor, Rimbaud thought, and put his mind to devising a proper method of entertaining the Roman Four trespasser. This, his initial act as host, might be an important occasion; future relations would probably depend on how he handled the first caller at Boxed M.

Rimbaud grinned, believing he had hit upon a fit reception. When he reached the lower slopes of the divide he turned south and rode for upwards of an hour, taking a roundabout course that eventually brought him to a mesquite-fringed wash a mile south of Maiben's yard. He couldn't see the ridge now, but reckoned it was due north of him, and that whoever was watching Sam's cabin wouldn't be expecting trouble from this direction.

The land here was rutted by dry washes running between Jigsaw Divide and the farther mesas. Rimbaud crossed two brush-tangled benches and negotiated a deep arroyo and another dry wash before reaching a vantage point that offered him a view of the ridge. For several minutes, while he studied that rock-ribbed elevation, he saw no sign of life. There was no repetition of the flash. Had the visitor departed? Or was his hunch wrong?

He was riding forward when he glimpsed a black horse that stood tied to a mesquite tree part way up the slope. And now, observing the long-shanked Spanish bit that glinted in the sunlight, Rimbaud smiled. Except for that silver-inlaid bit he might have ridden into ambush. Survival could depend on damned trivial things.

Although a patient scrutiny of the ridge disclosed no sign of the black's rider, Rimbaud felt confident that he could find him. The sneaking son would be forted up behind brush or boulders on top, where he could pick off a living target in the yard. That was the way these deals were invariably rigged. The names and places differed, but the bushwhack pattern remained unchanged. Dismounting, Rimbaud tied the roan to a clump of catclaw, took off his spurs, and hung them on the saddlehorn. Then, gun in hand, he moved cautiously up the ridge. When he came close to the black horse Rimbaud spoke quietly to the animal, which had a Roman Four brand on its left hip. Maneuvering around the horse, he searched for boot tracks and found them. A big man, judging by the size of his boots, and Rimbaud thought at once: Booger Bill.

This craft tracking of a hunter by the hunted was also part of the pattern; a trick Jim Rimbaud had used to good advantage on several occasions. There was no better place than behind the man who was hunting you. He grinned, recalling how he'd once trailed a tough bunch of Chisholm riders through timber for two days while they in turn followed his tracks in continuous circle.

Warily, with a calculating caution that guarded against stepping on a dead branch or scuffing a stone, Rimbaud followed the tracks through a screening growth of greasewood. When he was within a few yards of the crest he crouched low, inching forward with a patient stealth until he glimpsed the steepled crown of a gray hat directly ahead of him.

Rising to his full height now, Rimbaud saw a huge man hunkered behind a low barricade of rimrock. Coarse black hair hung down to the greasy collar of his tan shirt. He had been engaged in rolling a cigarette; now he thumbed a match aflame, lit his cigarette, and eased into a more comfortable position. Giving him a deliberate appraisal, Rimbaud observed that he wasn't wearing a holstered gun, which seemed odd. Then he saw a Winchester tilted against the rock outcrop with a shell-lined cartridge belt beside it.

As if sensing surveillance, the big man turned his head in the slow way of a ponderous range bull. When his broad-jawed face came around Rimbaud asked, "Are you Booger Bill?"

He nodded, and peered at Rimbaud's leveled gun. Revealing neither surprise nor anger, he got up, discarded the cigarette, and asked sullenly, "Who be you?"

"Name of Rimbaud."

Booger Bill stared at him, demanding, "Jim Rimbaud?"

"Yeah."

"But Lew said you was layin' drunk in town," Booger Bill objected.

Rimbaud eased around to the Winchester. "You

can't believe everything Stromberg tells you," he chided. "Lew is a great hand for funning."

"He wasn't funnin' me," Bill insisted solemnly. "Lew said you was drunk and wouldn't be out here for a couple days. Said you was on a rip-roarin' spree."

Recalling Limpy Smith's description of this Roman Four rider, Rimbaud marveled at its accuracy. Bill was so broad that he didn't appear tall, yet Rimbaud guessed him to be a full six feet. And as Smith had said, the big man seemed to be a trifle loco in the noggin.

"You're trespassing on private property," Rimbaud announced. "Get to hell off it."

Perspiration made its oily shine on the dark unchanging mask of Booger Bill's thick-muscled face. Even his muddy brown eyes seemed blank as he said, "You can't run me off. Sheriff Sol Robillarde swore me in as a deputy, which means I got a right to be here."

"To hell with that," Rimbaud said. "I'm telling you to vamoose."

When Booger Bill made no move to leave, Rimbaud waggled the gun and ordered harshly, "Go on. Drag your rump."

Booger Bill's face retained its congealed impassiveness, but now a wildness came into his eyes. He drew a deep breath that flared his nostrils and visibly expanded his massive chest. All the brute power of the man blazed in a queer red brilliance that stained his eyes as he bellowed, "Nobody runs me off, by God!"

Even then Rimbaud couldn't quite believe it, until Booger Bill lunged at him both huge fists cocked high like clubs poised for pounding.

He made a broad target for a bullet. And he was as violently destructive as an enraged bull. In this tumultuous moment there was no time for ethical reasoning; yet some inherent reluctance to shoot an unarmed man kept Jim Rimbaud from firing. Swiftly stepping aside, he slashed at Booger Bill's head with his gun barrel, struck a clubbed fist, and distinctly heard the crack of a bone breaking.

Booger Bill yelped a curse. He wheeled and charged again, shouting, "I'll stomp your goddamn guts into the ground!"

Calmly now, with the intent calculation of a man sledging a beef steer, Rimbaud hit him on the head. Dust puffed from the barrel-dented hat. Booger Bill staggered on for a few steps. He peered about in blind confusion and said thickly, "I'll stomp—"

Then his slack-jawed mouth sagged open and he went down in the slow, knee-bended fashion of a tired horse wanting to roll.

Rimbaud holstered his pistol. He picked up Bill's cartridge belt and buckled it around his hips, then examined the Winchester and found it fully loaded. He had lost a similar rifle in Mexico and thought: This will come in handy.

Then he stepped over to Booger Bill and nudged him with a boot, saying, "Wake up, bully boy. Wake up!"

Booger Bill grunted. His eyes opened and he blinked against the sunlight and demanded, "What's goin' on?"

"You are," Rimbaud said. He prodded Booger Bill with the Winchester and ordered, "Get off your rump and ride out of here."

Bill rubbed his head in the dazed way of a man awakening from a drunkard's dream. "I must of stubbed my toe on a rock," he muttered. Then memory came to him and he said, "You pistol-whipped me! That's what you done. Pistol-whipped me."

He held up his bruised left hand and peered at it.

"You busted my thumb," he accused.

"I'll bust your goddamn head too if you don't get a move on," Rimbaud warned without pity. His years of drifting and fighting had taught him to meet toughness with toughness; to match brutality with brutality. There was no place for tolerance or compassion in the gunsmoke game. It was punish or be punished, smash or be smashed; and God help the man who played it otherwise.

Booger Bill stood up. A sluggish, smoldering resentment showed in his eyes now, but the wildness was gone. He peered intently at Rimbaud for a moment, as if seeing him for the first time and wanting to remember him. Then he turned and walked down the ridge toward his horse.

Trailing along behind, Rimbaud watched Booger Bill support himself against the horse and vomit. When that was over the big man called, "I'll pay you back, Rimbaud."

Then he climbed clumsily into the saddle and rode southward, not looking back.

So now there's three of them wanting my scalp, Rimbaud thought. Link, Jubal, And Booger Bill. But it occurred to him that Lew Stromberg would probably hate him the most. And because there was a cautious streak in Stromberg, the Roman Four boss would be the most dangerous foe. You wouldn't catch Lew coming at an armed man with his bare fists, Rimbaud reasoned. Lew's temper would never prod him beyond the realm of reasonable risk. It didn't occur to Jim Rimbaud that he might have misjudged Stromberg, or that there'd come a time when he would be forced to revise his opinion of Della's father.

Mounting the roan, Rimbaud rode across the ridge and gave Maiben's place a casual appraisal. The long, dirt-roofed log cabin was flanked by a wagon shed and two corrals. Except for three tamarisk trees that shaded it on the west, the yard was free of growth and thus furnished fair protection against a sneak attack. A fly-swarmed quarter of beef hung in the wagon shed, two shrunk-up cowhides draped the corral fence, and tin cans littered one side of the yard.

"Not much of an outfit," Rimbaud reflected. But presently, as he explored the cabin, he found the two rooms surprisingly well furnished. The kitchen, with its cupboard shelves neatly trimmed by scalloped red oilcloth and white curtains at the window, revealed a woman's knack for frilly fixings. The other room contained a huge four-poster bed, an ornately carved bureau with a large mirror, three comfortable chairs, and a varnished commode. A stone fireplace, flanked by filled book shelves, formed one end of the room, and there were colorful drapes at the window.

Eve's doings, Rimbaud guessed, and thought how it would be with her here. One hour with Eve would turn this cabin into a king's palace. He wondered if a wedding date had been set, and for the first time in his life was envious of another man's possessions.

Slicing meat from the quarter of beef, Rimbaud cooked a meal and ate it without relish. The thought came to him that a man shouldn't have to eat supper alone, or sit listening with a loaded rifle beside his chair. The gunsmoke game was all right for young bucks wanting adventure and a reputation. They could take the loneliness, knowing there'd be booze and flirty females in town to make up for it. But there came a time when a man got over that. He got his fill of fighting, and fancy women, and aimless wandering. A time came when he wanted his own home and a sweet-loving wife to share it.

"Must be getting old," Rimbaud said, and was

shocked at the realization. It had never occurred to him that the seven short years that separated twenty-eight from twenty-one could make that much difference.

At dusk he sat on the cabin's front steep with the Winchester near at hand. Three horses, two bays and a paint, had come in from the horse trap for their evening drink at the water trough. They stood near the corral gate for half an hour, enviously watching the roan munch hay; then they departed in single file, their shadowy shapes merging into the mauve dusk.

A cow's plaintive bawling made a mournful sound against the vast silence, and presently Rimbaud heard a remote rumor of hoofbeats off to the southwest. Della heading homeward, he supposed, and wondered how she kept her romantic trysts with Maiben a secret from her father. Lew Stromberg would be outraged if he knew his daughter was supplying Maiben with food. And what would Eve's reaction be if she learned her future husband was accepting favors from a big-breasted teaser?

"An odd deal all around," Rimbaud muttered.

When full darkness came he went to the haystack and toted hay to a wagon in the shed, then brought blankets from the cabin. The wagon might not be as comfortable as that four-poster bed, but it would be a safer place to sleep if Roman Four riders staged a night raid. And they would, eventually.

CHAPTER EIGHT

A Sabbath hush had cloaked Spanish Strip's timbered hills and long meadows all day. Except for tenuous spirals of dust rising occasionally, there was no sign of travel across the wide benchland between Isabelle's Camp on the east and the Pothole country to the west. But because Swede Severide understood that not all the spirals were kicked up by dust devils, he kept a patient watch from his tree-shaded veranda throughout the afternoon.

"They'd better not show themselves around here, those Roman Four toughs," Swede muttered when his wife came out to change the wet pack on his bruised head. "I've took all I'm going to take."

His son Oscar, who would be eight come calf-roundup time, bragged, "I'll help you with my slingshot, Daddy. I'll shoot them in the eye."

Whereupon ten-year-old Jan scoffed, "What darn good is a measly little slingshot?" He honed the blade of his newly acquired knife and announced, "I could cut their gizzards out with this, it's so sharp."

"That's no fit way to talk on Sunday," Ingrid Severide objected. She possessed a pious devotion to religious principles that no amount of persecution could shake. Right was right, to her way of thinking, and anything less was wrong. "This is the

83

Lord's day and should be set aside for peaceful thoughts," she insisted.

"You might try telling that to Stromberg's bunch," Swede suggested. "They ride the same on Sunday as any other time, and their thoughts are not peaceable."

Then he smiled, remembering what had happened to Ernie Link and Hugh Jubal last night. "That Jim Rimbaud gave them their needings," he mused. "Rimbaud is wilder than they are."

"Is he wilder than you?" Jan asked, and when his father didn't answer, demanded, "He's not wilder than you, is he, Daddy?"

"Of course he is," Mrs. Severide said, "Your father is no wild, gun-shooting man. He is a respectable, God-fearing husband and father who should set a fit example for his sons."

"Such as turning the other cheek?" Swede asked moodily. "The Christ did that, and they crucified him."

"Torsten Severide!" she exclaimed. "You should not speak so of the Savior!"

But Swede said stubbornly, "It is true, Ingrid. He did not fight and he was crucified."

Shortly after sundown Maria Bonn went to the corral where her husband was saddling his horse. She handed him a burlap bag partly filled with provisions, saying, "That will keep Sam from starving for a day or two, if you find him."

"Not so loud," Bonn cautioned, and gave the dusk-veiled yard a probing scrutiny. "I've got a feeling somebody is close by."

When he climbed into the saddle Maria said, "You be careful, Charley." Apprehension got the better of her now and she exclaimed, "I don't like for you to be rimming around in the dark! What if they should mistake you for Sam Maiben and start

84

shooting at you?"

"Hush, woman—hush," Bonn commanded.

But Maria asked, "Where will it end, all this dodging and conniving? Sam can't stay hid forever. There's got to be an accounting sometime."

"Sure, and we'll have Jim Rimbaud to help us when that time comes," Bonn said confidently. He patted her shoulder and whispered, "Don't fret about me, Maria. I'll be all right."

Maria reached up and rubbed his knee, which was the most intimate gesture she had made since their baby boy had died ten years ago. "You be careful, Charley."

"Sure," Bonn said. He was out in the sandy road, riding at a walk and making no noise at all when Hugh Jubal demanded, "Where you goin', Bonn?"

Charley peered at the indistinct shape of Roman Four's ramrod and considered his chances of giving Jubal the slip. It wouldn't be difficult in this moonless gloom; just a matter of whirling his horse off into the timber. But Jubal was a bad one to fool with. He probably had a gun in his hand.

Bonn sighed, choosing the cautious way, as he had so many times when challenged by Stromberg's riders. "Might be going to Isabelle's Camp," he muttered with an honest man's dislike for telling an outright lie.

"What for?" Jubal asked suspiciously, and when Bonn didn't answer, demanded, "What would you be goin' there for at this time of night?"

"Well, my woman might have a toothache, and I might be going after a bottle of arnica to rub on her jaw."

Bonn thought it sounded convincing, and quite logical. But Jubal said. "I might ride along with you, to make sure."

And he did.

Five miles to the southeast, Roman Four's Buck Aubrey stood behind a woodpile in Al Shumway's yard and watched a wagon roll past the lamplit kitchen doorway with four of the Shumways in it. He listened to the diminishing rumble of wheels and decided the wagon was headed toward Swenson's ranch; then he led his horse around so that he could look into the kitchen, where sixteen-year-old Ruth Shumway was washing supper dishes.

She wore a red satin blouse that emphasized the golden sheen of her wheat-straw hair, and a frilly apron that fitted her slim hips snugly. Watching her walk between table and sink, and guessing why she had remained here alone, Buck smiled. There wasn't a prettier girl in all Quadrille Basin, to his way of thinking. Or one half so sweet.

Leading his horse around to the front of the house, Aubrey called, "How's for a cup of coffee?"

Ruth came to the doorway at once. "Buck!" she said happily. "I'm so glad you've come!"

When he came into the kitchen she had coffee and chocolate cake waiting for him on the table.

"I'm supposed to be on the move betwixt here and Swenson's," Buck reported, smoothing down his rebellious brown hair. "But I got hungry, watchin' you in here all by yourself."

"Oh, so it's just the food that attracted you," Ruth accused with mock concern.

Buck shook his head. "You know better'n that."

"No, I don't," Ruth denied.

This was the first time Buck Aubrey had set foot in the house, or in the yard, for that matter. They'd met out beyond the corral on three Sunday nights in succession, and occasionally in other places. But being here in the house with her was different, somehow. It made him feel a trifle uneasy, as if Al Shumway might be watching what went on.

"I'd sure dislike to have your folks catch me in here," he admitted.

Ruth giggled. "Ma would have a conniption fit. She thinks a girl my age shouldn't even look at a man, much less talk to him. I guess she's forgotten how it was when she was sixteen."

"Suppose," Buck agreed, still standing just inside the doorway, hat in hand.

"I'm glad you didn't get hurt in town last night, like Ernie Link did," Ruth said. "When the shooting started I was afraid it might be you."

Buck shrugged, taking no pride in the part he had played. "Ernie should of knowed better than to mess with Jim Rimbaud," he muttered. "If it wasn't for me wantin' to see you tonight, I'd of asked to go on that beef gather across the line with the West Camp crew. I got no hankerin' to tangle with Rimbaud. None at all."

Ruth motioned for him to sit down at the table. "That's all you came for," she teased. "Just to eat."

Buck wished they were out in the brush behind the corral. He didn't like to think what might happen if her father should catch him here. Or worse yet, if her high-toned mother caught him. Mrs. Shumway had a sharp tongue and was a leader in the Junction church. She'd think he wasn't fit for Ruth to wipe her feet on. But even so, Buck couldn't resist the invitation in Ruth's lamplit eyes. He reached out and took her in his arms and kissed her till she was gasping for breath.

"Do you still think it was just food I wanted?" he demanded.

Ruth was blushing now, her girlish bosom lifting and lowering with the ebb and flow of her excited breathing. "I knew what you wanted," she said. Then she asked worriedly, "Whatever will we do about it, Buck?"

Which was a question young Aubrey couldn't answer.

Jim Rimbaud awoke a daybreak, fully rested. He had fed his horse and was making a fire in the kitchen stove when the roan nickered. Whirling instantly, Rimbaud picked up the Winchester. He stepped over to one side of the doorway and saw his horse standing at the corral gate, its ears pricked forward.

Somebody coming from the east, Rimbaud thought. Going outside, he kept close to the cabin wall until he could see around the corner. A single rider, coming slowly across the mesquite-blotched flats, was barely visible against the shadowy bulk of Jigsaw Divide, which reared high behind him. Rimbaud was reasonably sure that it was Sam Maiben, wanting a cup of coffee at his own table. But he waited until he could definitely identify the oncoming horseman before returning to the kitchen.

Maiben, he reflected, was taking a long chance coming here in daylight. For all Sam knew, Booger Bill might be out there on the ridge right now, waiting to catch him in his rifle sights. But a man could get fed up with skulking around the rimrock by himself. Especially a homesteader accustomed to a comfortable bed.

Rimbaud had the coffeepot on and bacon frying in a skillet when Maiben rode into the yard. A faint grin creased Maiben's bearded cheeks as he got down, announcing, "The prodigal son returns." His red-rimmed eyes warily raked the yonder trees and he asked, "Anybody around last night?"

"No," Rimbaud said, standing in the doorway. "Did they bother you?"

Maiben shook his head. "But I didn't sleep, regardless. Not a wink."

He led 'his horse over to the corral, unsaddled, and forked it a feed of hay. When he came into the kitchen he said wearily, "This dodging ain't no fun, for a fact."

"Even with a pretty girl to keep you company?" Rimbaud asked slyly.

Maiben didn't like that and showed it in the quick way he said, "Della didn't stay long." He watched Rimbaud pour coffee, adding, "She's a trifle on the flirty side, but it don't mean a thing."

Rimbaud grinned. "It might mean something to Lew Stromberg if he caught her," he suggested.

"I tried to tell her that. But she's all mixed up with romantic notions about the way folks should live. She read a lot of books at that school in Tucson. Poetry and such. According to her theory, folks pay too much attention to making money and not enough to living. She says her old man thinks more of cattle than he does of people."

"Shouldn't wonder," Rimbaud reflected.

Maiben sat down and blew steam from his coffee. Then, as the two roans started a commotion in the corral, he jumped up, tipping over his chair and clawing for his gun.

"Just our ponies trying each other out for size," Rimbaud said. Seeing the tension ebb from Maiben's haggard face, he added, "You're spooky as a bunch-quitter bronc."

"It's the listening," Maiben said. "The goddamn listening. I listen all the time."

He reached behind some staples on a bottom shelf and brought out a gallon jug. He pulled the cork, tilted the jug expertly, and took a long drink. "Snake-bite medicine," he said. "Want a swig?"

Rimbaud grimaced, the thought of whisky before breakfast was hugely distasteful to him. "Don't like the stuff that well," he said.

Maiben took another drink before putting the

89

jug away in its hiding place. "I'm supposed to be a teetotaler," he admitted with a sly wink. "A feller who never takes a drink—not even a glass of beer. Folks would sure be surprised to know I keep a jug in the house. But there's times when a man needs a drink real bad. Like now."

He sat down and loosed a gusty sigh and began eating. But his bloodshot eyes didn't relax. They kept shifting furtively from window to doorway. He was like a tight-strung wire vibrating to the slightest sound. Rimbaud understood how it was with him. A man got that way when constant pressure keyed his nerves too high. He got so he couldn't relax, day or night. It occurred to Rimbaud now that he should feel sorry for this homesteader who'd once saved his life: Maiben couldn't be blamed for asking Eve Odegarde to marry him, or for the fact that she had accepted his proposal while a fiddlefooted drifter was off making horse tracks in the dust. But even so, understanding how unfair it was, Rimbaud couldn't discard his resentment.

Maiben poured himself a second cup of coffee. He said, "This is the first time I ever had to dodge the law. By God, I hope it's the last."

Afterward, as he shaved at the sink, he asked, "Do you know Eve Odegarde?" When Rimbaud nodded, Maiben said, "We planned to get married next month. Had our plans all set. Eve moved some of her furniture in here. I think I'll go to town and have a talk with her, after dark. Maybe I'll give myself up and stand trial, if she thinks that's the thing to do."

"Any way of proving you got framed?" Rimbaud inquired.

Maiben shook his head. "The deal will be rigged against me right from the start. The circuit judge is a friend of Stromberg's and so is Sheriff Robillarde. Sol wants to be a big politician, and stands a chance of going to Prescott next year. He's honest enough. I don't think Sol would deliberately frame a man. But he sure won't give me none the best of it in court."

"Do you figure Stromberg planted that Roman Four yearling on your range himself?" Rimbaud asked.

"No. Hugh Jubal probably did the dirty work. Della says she heard her father tell Jubal a week ago that he had to get the goods on me or find a new job. Lew has hated my guts ever since Eve and I started keeping company. He wanted her himself."

"I can understand that," Rimbaud reflected.

Maiben eyed him sharply, asking, "You friendly with Eve?"

Rimbaud smiled and said, "Friendly enough to know she's an attractive woman."

Maiben thought about that in frowning silence for a moment. He glanced at the bottom shelf, where the jug was hidden, and said, "I wouldn't want her to know about me having whisky in the house. She's dead set against booze. Her old man turned into a terrible drunkard, and Eve won't have anything to do with a man who drinks."

The bald hypocrisy of it shocked Jim Rimbaud. Maiben not only admitted winning Eve's favor by false pretense, but seemed to think it was reasonable and right to do so. It occurred to Rimbaud now that a man who'd cheat the woman he was going to marry might also steal cattle. He asked, "Are you telling it straight, about that altered brand?" ·

"What do you mean—straight?"

"I mean did you do it yourself?" Rimbaud said bluntly.

Maiben grinned. He said, "You're the first of my

91

friends to doubt me."

"I'm not your friend," Rimbaud said, wanting this understood. "I'm just a galoot who owes you a debt, and I'm paying it."

"Well, I didn't have anything to do with that particular calf," Maiben announced. "I've hair-branded a few that might've strayed away from Roman Four cows, and caught myself a maverick now and then, like everyone else. But I didn't change that brand." Then he asked, "What difference would it make to you, one way or the other?"

"Not much," Rimbaud admitted, knowing that this talk wouldn't alter his obligation to pay the debt he owed Maiben. "But if a man is innocent of the crime he's charged with, there's always a bare chance it can be proved."

Maiben shrugged and said wearily, "I don't see how, Jim. I just don't see how."

Neither did Rimbaud. But he asked, "Do you think Lew Stromberg knows that Jubal framed you?"

"Not for sure," Maiben said thoughtfully. "Lew is slick when it comes to keeping out of trouble with the law. He wouldn't let even his own foreman get anything on him. It's my guess that Jubal drove that calf up here, used a cinch ring to reburn its brand into what looked like a Boxed M, and then hightailed to tell Sheriff Robillarde that he had the goods on me. It was just an accident that they caught me skinning the damn critter."

He walked to the doorway and said again, "I don't see how in hell it could be proved. Nobody saw Jubal do it, and he'd never tell on himself. So how could you convince a court of law that it's a damned dirty frame-up?"

Jim Rimbaud was thinking about that as he

watched Maiben ride off a few moments later. Truth might not count for much in court, but sometimes it could be used as a club against a guilty man. If Hugh Jubal had altered that brand, there might be a way to force a confession out of him.

Sunlight spilled over the crest of Jigsaw Divide while Rimbaud sat on the front stoop and contemplated the possibility of clearing Maiben of the rustling charge. It seemed almost hopeless, as Sam had said. For Hugh Jubal wouldn't be caught easy, or confess easy. And now, recalling Maiben's reference to his marriage plans, Rimbaud thought: Why in hell should I try to clear him?

Day's heat built up and became a brassy glare that shimmered across the brush-blotched flats. Rimbaud kept a wary watch to the southwest, believing that when trouble came it would come from that direction. But there was another kind of trouble and it was here already—a nagging devil of discontent that kept intruding upon his thoughts; that kept pecking at him like a fly at a festered sore. It told him that Sam Maiben couldn't get married while he was dodging a posse or serving time in prison. The way Sam was now, with his nerves tied in knots, he might even decide to leave the country. Eve wouldn'd go with him, the devil assured; she wouldn't marry a quitter. A smart man might catch her on the rebound; might make her forget there'd ever been a homesteader named Sam Maiben.

But there was another devil—a jeering, scoffing imp that roosted somewhere inside Rimbaud's head and reminded him that Maiben had saved his life. You're going through the motions of paying a debt, this devil taunted, but because you want his woman you won't help Sam clear his name.

Rimbaud swore softly and tried to discard the

nagging devils of discontent. Hell, he was doing what he'd been asked to do, he told himself. All he could be expected to do. It wasn't his fault that Maiben had got himself into a tight place, and it wouldn't be his fault if Maiben went to prison on a trumped-up charge. It wasn't as if the man had never stolen; Sam had admitted taking other Roman Four calves. He was no lily, by any means.

But even so, Rimbaud couldn't quite convince his conscience, or shrug off the sense of shame that clung to him. Maiben hadn't asked any questions about *his* morals the night he'd picked up a blood-sapped stranger. Nor had he inquired about his romantic notions. In fact, Maiben had probably guessed he was aiding a fugitive, either from the law or an irate husband. He'd had no way of knowing his unconscious passenger was a survivor of the Murphy-Chisholm feud.

"All he did," Rimbaud mused, "was save my life."

And presently, as he saddled the roan, Rimbaud thought: If Jubal was caught he could be made to talk, one way or another.

CHAPTER NINE

Lew Stromberg couldn't understand it. His crew had ridden half the night and watched every homestead on the Spanish Strip without catching Sam Maiben. Booger Bill, supposed to be the best tracker in Quadrille Basin, had not only failed to find the Boxed M rustler, but had come home half drunk with a bandaged hand and a garbled account of being pistol-whipped by Jim Rimbaud.

Everything, it seemed to Stromberg, had gone haywire these past few days: Francisco Durango's death, the crew's failure to catch Maiben, and Jim Rimbaud's loco decision to guard Boxed M. Even Della, who's always been a trifle on the rebellious side, was brazenly refusing to obey him. Ordered to remain at the ranch, she went traipsing off in all directions the moment his back was turned. On top of all this, Eve Odegarde wouldn't so much as speak to him. He had tried to explain that there was no doubt about Maiben's guilt, but she wouldn't even listen. She'd walked away from him without so much as a word. It was enough to make a man bog his head.

For the first time in his life Lew Stromberg felt the tight grip of enormous frustration, of being thwarted by circumstances that he could neither control nor avoid. All morning, while the crew caught up on sleep, he had endeavored to puzzle out the flaw; to identify the reason his carefully plotted plans for Roman Four's future were producing continued failure. There must be some reason for all this damned mix-up. Nothing like it had ever happened to him before. Every move he made was blocked, somehow. Even Sol Robillarde, who'd been his good friend ever since becoming sheriff, was warning him to watch his step.

Something was wrong, sure as hell. But think as he might, there seemed to be no logical answer. Every move he'd made, except for allowing Ernie Link to try a shoot-out with Rimbaud, had been deliberately weighed and cloaked with legality. Every single, solitary move, including his revenge against Sam Maiben. No court of law would question his right to hunt down a cow thief, or fail to convict on such evidence of guilt. But the thieving bastard had to be caught first.

That was the thing that astonished Lew Stromberg, the thing that wholly confused him. Even thought it had been necessary to send half his crew to Sonora, there should have been enough men to capture Maiben. Men to spare. The dirty son had to eat. He couldn't just squat in the shade of a mesquite like a hibernating snake. Maiben had to find food and water; had to move from one place to another. Yet he hadn't been caught.

Now, as Lew Stromberg rode northward with six men at noon, he muttered sourly, "One shiftless homesteader making suckers of my whole headquarters crew. It's enough to turn a man's stomach. By God, I should fire the bunch of you and hire some real hands."

Hugh Jubal, still smarting from his inglorious defeat of Saturday night, said, "Maybe Maiben sneaked into Junction and hid out at Eve Odegarde's."

Stromberg rejected that by announcing, "Sol

Robillarde and Ernie are keeping a day-and-night watch between them in town. That's why Sol isn't out in the hills looking for Maiben. I told him we'd do the riding—and the finding, if Maiben didn't run into town."

"Sam has just been downright lucky," Jubal complained. "Chances are he'd of got caught last night if Rimbaud hadn't run Bill off the ridge at Boxed M. I'd bet a month's pay that Maiben ate supper with Rimbaud at his own table while the rest of us was watchin' them other places. It stands to reason Sam must of ate somewheres."

Booger Bill glared at him. "Rimbaud busted my thumb," he said sullenly, and stuck out his bandaged left hand in evidence. "I had to git it fixed, didn't I?"

"But you could of let us know," Hugh Jubal complained, "instead of spendin' a whole evenin' at the Shiloh bar lappin' up beer. If you'd of just tipped us off, we'd of took a look at Maiben's place last night."

Lew Stromberg made a derisive, chopping motion at Jubal. "Don't pass the blame to him. It was your fault for not sending another man down there to see how things were going. I told you to keep the crew moving and cover all that country, hour in and hour out. I thought you could understand plain English. Instead of me going to West Camp, I should've sent you, and done my own ramrodding. I'll know better next time, by God!"

Hugh Jubal hung his head. Getting dressed down in front of the men was nothing new. But it wasn't a nice thing to take, and there were times, like now, when he wondered if those few extra dollars he got for being foreman were worth it. He'd always wanted to be ramrod of a big outfit. All his life he'd itched to be the boss of a rough crew, to give orders and have the fine feeling that he was a cut above the common bunch. Now he wasn't so sure.

Presently, as they rode into a dry wash some three miles west of Maiben's place, Stromberg called a halt. In the fashion of a roundup boss sending out circle riders, he split the crew, telling Jubal, Red Shafter, and Booger Bill to watch Boxed M. "Now don't go making targets of yourselves," he warned. "I'm short one man already. Just be damned sure that Maiben doesn't get his supper there tonight."

"You still want him took alive?" Jubal asked.

Stromberg nodded. "That's how I prefer it," he said. "Of course, it may not be possible, and I want him grabbed even if you have to fill him full of lead to do it. But I'll pay a hundred-dollar bonus if he's taken alive."

It was significant that none of these men took the liberty of asking why their boss wanted Maiben captured alive. Hugh Jubal could make a good guess, knowing how Lew felt about Eve Odegarde. But Mike Flanagan and Ray Slade, who'd been at the Pothole line camp for two years, wouldn't know about Stromberg's romantic notions. Nor did Booger Bill, who eyed Stromberg with unconcealed wonderment, yet refrained from blurting the question that puzzled him.

Lew Stromberg's word was law. This dark saturnine man was king here, and his commands weren't to be questioned. He seldom bothered to explain his decisions, having an aristocrat's contempt for hired hands. But now, sensing the crew's curiosity, Stromberg said, "It would be worth a hundred dollars to see Maiben behind bars. A dead homesteader might look like a hero to some folks. Especially to women. But a jailbird is no hero to anyone. He's just a fool who got himself caught."

"I figgered that was it," Jubal said, a self-satisfied smile rutting his sorrel-stubbled cheeks. "By grab, I knowed it."

Stromberg eyed him arrogantly and demanded, "Anything odd about my opinion?"

"No," Hugh said meekly. "Not a thing, Boss. It was just that I had it figgered out in advance."

"First time I ever heard of a doorknob figuring," Stromberg said sourly.

Red Shafter laughed, poking a finger at Jubal and saying, "A doorknob with ears." Then he asked, "How about Rimbaud, Boss?"

Stromberg thought about it for a moment before saying, "We'll run him off, when the sign is right. But if Rimbaud got shot at Maiben's place now, it would put Sol Robillarde in a bad spot, with the territorial elections coming up."

"What difference does that make?" Shafter asked.

"The difference between having the law with Roman Four or against it," Stromberg explained. "You aren't working for a greasy-sack outfit that can pick up and run when it gets into law trouble. I co-operate with Robillarde one hundred per cent, which is why there'll be no legal opposition to Roman Four using some of this Strip graze for winter range."

"We could use it right now," Mike Flanagan suggested.

And Ray Slade said, "Them steers around the Potholes will be chawin' off each other's tails in another month. That country is ate down to the nubbin."

"I know," Stromberg said irritably. "But we'll do first things first." Realizing that Buck Aubrey hadn't spoken, he asked, "What you so quiet about today, kid?"

Buck shook his head, not speaking, and Red Shafter said, "He's still scairt, thinkin' how he held a gun on Jim Rimbaud."

"He should of pulled the trigger," Jubal muttered, "while he had the drop."

Stromberg peered at his foreman and demanded, "Do you understand your instructions?"

"Well, you want Maiben ketched, alive or otherwise, and no shooting with Rimbaud until later on."

Stromberg nodded and rode off, followed by Aubrey, Flanagan, and Slade.

Booger Bill fell in behind Shafter and Jubal, who headed eastward along the wash. "If I could git my hands on Rimbaud I'd stomp his guts into the ground," he muttered.

"Lew would like that," Jubal said, "and so would I. But how you goin' to ketch a gun-slinger like Rimbaud without shootin' him first?"

"It might be done," Red Shafter suggested, "if we go at it right, and have a little luck."

At about this same time Jim Rimbaud completed half of a wide circle that had given him glimpses of two homesteads and the little settlement called Isabelle's Camp. He rode slowly, keeping off the trails and reading their sign of recent travel when he crossed them. There had been a considerable amount of riding through this country last night. He smiled, thinking that those patrols had been seeking a fugitive who'd been furnished his supper by Lew Stromberg's daughter. What a joke that was!

Near midafternoon Rimbaud came to Al Shumway's alfalfa patch, where the toil-warped homesteader was irrigating with water ditched from a windmill tank.

"Git down and rest your saddle," Shumway invited, and offered Rimbaud his Durham sack.

Rimbaud got down, shaped a cigarette, and

squatted on his heels for a smoke. "Whose place is that off to the west?" he inquired.

"Swede Severide's," Shumway said, "and the one south of it is Charlie Bonn's."

"You have a visitor last night?" Rimbaud asked.

Shumway shook his head.

"Well, according to the sign, somebody rode into your yard," Rimbaud said. He glanced at the house, wondering if Shumway had a young wife, or a daughter. Then he said, "Looks like somebody has ridden up to that patch of brush behind your corral a half-dozen times lately."

"That so?" Shumway asked. "Well, it's news to me. I'll keep watch tonight and see what's goin' on."

Then, canting his head for a look at the sun, he said, "Won't be long till suppertime. Stop by and take potluck with us."

It was a temptation, and the thought of eating a woman-cooked meal made Rimbaud's mouth water. But he said, "Reckon I better not. It wouldn't be fitting for Roman Four to come calling at Maiben's place and me not be there to welcome them."

Shumway chuckled. "You figger they might come this evenin'?"

Rimbaud shrugged and climbed into his saddle. "No telling when," he said quietly. "But they'll come, and it's my guess they'll come after dark."

"Good luck," Shumway called. "If you need anythin', just let me know."

Rimbaud smiled thinly. There'd be no time to ask for what he would be needing.

Again, as he had this morning, Rimbaud contemplated the chances of catching Hugh Jubal and forcing a confession out of him. The Roman Four ramrod had probably been on patrol last night, and would be again this evening. But meeting up with him after dark would be a matter of blind luck. There was only one sure place to find him—at Roman Four. And a man might not survive the meeting.

As Rimbaud crossed a rock-ribbed strip of benchland just north of Boxed M, a cow's steady bawling attracted his attention. The critter's complaint reminded him of boyhood days when he'd ridden bog each spring. It held the same note of bovine desperation. There probably wasn't a boggy slough in all Quadrille Basin, but something ailed the cow. So thinking, Rimbaud turned his horse and presently glimpsed a brindle calf lying beside a brush-fringed rock outcrop. Newborn, he guessed, and now saw that there was a motley-faced brindle cow standing behind it in the brush.

The scrawny calf got part way up, then collapsed.

"Starved," Rimbaud muttered, and was wondering why a calf should go hungry with its mother alive when he observed that the cow had got her hindquarters wedged in a narrow crevasse between two shelves of faulted rock. Even though her front legs were free, the cow couldn't get out, and the calf couldn't nurse.

Remembering that he'd heard a cow bawling last night, Rimbaud unlatched his catch rope. He rode close, dropped a loop over the cow's scrawny hips, and fashioned a squaw hitch. Then, taking his dallies, Rimbaud sent his horse ahead. The rope tightened around the cow's rump, and as the lifting pull hoisted her to the top of the crevasse, Rimbaud reined his horse off at a sharp angle.

The cow fell sideways, barely missing the prone calf. Rimbaud shook off the loop, observing a Boxed M on the brindle's hip as she scrambled to her feet. Except for the fact that her slat-ribbed sides and hind legs were rubbed raw, she seemed all right. But the little bull calf, which was half dead from starvation, wouldn't be able to follow its mother for forage and water.

"Coyote bait, unless he's corralled," Rimbaud reflected.

Dismounting and using his coiled rope as a weapon against the wild-eyed cow, he picked up the calf, hoisted it to his saddle, and balanced it there while he mounted. Then, with the calf cradled in his arms and the cow bawling motherly protests, he rode toward Boxed M.

It was coming sundown when Rimbaud entered the yard followed by the bellowing brindle. The thought had occurred to him that this noisy approach might be dangerous if Roman Four were on the prowl today. He had even considered abandoning the calf, but instead he had bowed to the strict code of cattleland, which prompted a man to take care of stock come hell or high water and regardless of risk to himself. It was a basic ingredient, this habit of caring for the cattle; a deep-rooted characteristic bred into generations of cow-country Texans.

Rimbaud was at the corral gate, endeavoring to dismount without dumping the calf, when Hugh Jubal shouted, "We got you covered, Rimbaud!"

Caught completely unprepared, Rimbaud turned to see Jubal step out of the wagon shed with a gun in his hand. At this same moment, as Booger Bill's huge shape emerged from behind the haystack, Red Shafter came from the cabin and called tauntingly, "You're just in time for supper."

Rimbaud glanced about the yard and asked, "Only three of you?"

When Jubal nodded, Rimbaud said, "Seems like you're taking quite a risk, Hugh, coming here practically alone."

"Smart-alecky, ain't you?" Jubal snapped, lifting Rimbaud's pistol from its holster and tossing it across the yard. "Well, you won't be long. I've got you right where I want you, Rimbaud. Just like we planned it. You'll be a tame rooster when we git through—tame as a hand-fed pigeon, by God!"

Rimbaud shrugged. This, he understood, was the price a man paid for sheer carelessness. Instead of making a wary circle to scout for sign of ambush, he had ridden in here with a calf in his arms, defenseless as a handcuffed sheepherder. And as witless. In these first moments he had no awareness of being afraid. The gut-clutch of fear would come to him presently, but right now he felt ashamed.

"Git down," Jubal ordered. He winked at Booger Bill and said with exaggerated politeness, "You two gents has met before, ain't you?"

"Yeah," Booger Bill mumbled, a hot expectancy in his eyes. "We met."

Rimbaud balanced the calf, stepped from the saddle, and carried it into the corral. When the mother cow trotted in he closed the gate and forked hay over the fence before asking, "What you got in mind, Jubal?"

Jubal's bruised face creased into a sly smile. He gently rubbed his swollen, discolored nose and said, "A little fun."

Jim Rimbaud made his guess as to what that meant, and saw it substantiated in the glinting expectancy of Booger Bill's eyes. But he asked rankly, "What the hell you mean by that?"

Jubal winked at his two companions and said triumphantly, "He's deef, boys. The poor feller don't hear good. And he don't shape near so high without his gun. In fact, he looks downright puny."

Then Jubal turned his hate-scorched eyes on Rimbaud and shouted, "Just a little fun!"

104

CHAPTER TEN

Standing with his back to the corral, Jim Rimbaud hung onto the pitchfork. It wasn't much of a weapon against men with guns, but if his hunch were correct, they weren't intending to shoot him. Not until Hugh Jubal had his fun. Booger Bill also would want revenge. Rimbaud glanced at the big man's bandaged hand and took frugal comfort in the thought that Bill could hit him with one fist only.

"Put down the pitchfork," ordered Jubal.

Rimbaud shook his head.

"Do like I tell you!" Jubal shouted arrogantly. "Don't you know I'm boss here?"

"Go to hell," Rimbaud muttered.

"I can make him drop it," offered Red Shafter eagerly. "I'll bust his arm with a bullet, like he done to Ernie."

And the way he smiled, with his lips tight across his teeth, told Rimbaud that he meant it. Red was the gun-slinger of this trio, the itchy-fingered one. He was proud of his shooting skill and eager to display it.

Jubal peered at Rimbaud and asked, "You want it shot out of your hands?"

"Sure he does," said Shafter, and tilted up his gun like a man preparing for target practice.

A forty-five with a cut-off barrel, Rimbaud

thought, eying the sightless, snub-nosed muzzle. A gun meant for head-to-head shooting; meant for killing.

There was a moment, seemingly endless, when Rimbaud held his breath; when the cocking mechanism of Shafter's gun sounded loud against the yard's silence. There was a timeless, gut-clutching interval of expectancy while Hugh Jubal peered at him through slitted eyes and Booger Bill spat out an amber stream of tobacco juice that made a distinct *plop* in the dust.

"I'll make a Christian out of you," Red bragged. "A one-armed Scripture-spoutin' Christian."

He glanced at Jubal, asking, "Shall I let him have it?"

Jubal's calculating gaze continued uninterrupted by the question. He was waiting for the tension to show, Rimbaud guessed; waiting for the pressure to do its work. Hugh understood what pressure could do to a man. He'd found out at the Shiloh Saturday night.

"How about it?" Red asked impatiently. "I can bust his arm with one slug."

"Not yet," Jubal muttered, revealing his annoyance in the way he added, "He's lived on frijoles and mescal so long they've turned him loco. You can't scare a goddamn lunatic. They got no sense."

He stood there for a moment, eying the pitchfork, then said, "You and Bill bring out the horses."

"What in hell for?" Shafter demanded.

Jubal chuckled, plainly pleased with himself now. "You'd never guess in a month of Sundays," he said secretively. "I got a little game in mind."

"What you talkin' about?" Booger Bill asked.

"*Juego de gallo*," Jubal announced smilingly.

"Game of the rooster," Red mused. "You mean with ropes?"

Jubal nodded. As Shafter and Bill hurried toward the wagon shed he bragged, "There's more'n one way to catch a smart-alecky rooster, by God!"

Rimbaud knew the game. He'd seen it many times in Mexico. It was a favorite event at San Juan's Day celebrations, wherein roosters were buried in dirt so that only their necks and heads were exposed as targets for wild riding *vaqueros* who reached down as they raced past, attempting to grasp the luckless birds . . .

"You don't look so brash now," Jubal derided.

Rimbaud knew he couldn't evade three ropes. Not for very long. He thought: There'll never be a better chance than now. He waited a moment longer, until Booger Bill and Red went into the wagon shed. Then, still clutching the pitchfork, he ran toward his horse, which stood nearby with dangling reins. If he could get into that saddle there'd be a slight chance.

Jubal wheeled swiftly to cut him off, dodged back as Rimbaud stabbed at him with the pitchfork, then fired his gun. That first slug, whanging past Rimbaud's shoulder and splintering a board in the corral gate, told Rimbaud how hopeless this deal was. But he kept on and was reaching for the roan's reins when Jubal's second bullet sliced a raw furrow across the animal's rump. The roan plunged past Rimbaud in squealing terror and narrowly avoided collision with Red Shafter who led two saddled horses from the wagon shed.

Rimbaud knew he was licked. He knew there wasn't one chance in a hundred to avoid the brutal banquet Hugh Jubal intended to serve him. Yet even now, understanding how futile further resistance would be, he backed to the corral fence and stood there grimly clutching the pitchfork.

"Smart, ain't you!" Jubal jeered. "So goddamn

107

smart you almost got yourself shot!"

Rimbaud shrugged. There was only one thing he could do now—attempt to fight them off until dark. But even that seemed wholly futile, for then he'd have to dodge bullets instead of ropes. He watched the three of them climb into their saddles and shake out their loops; saw the bright shine of anticipation in Hugh Jubal's eyes. The Roman Four ramrod was enjoying this, Rimbaud realized; it salved Hugh's pride for the beating he'd taken in town.

"Catch him by the neck and make him squawk," Jubal suggested happily. Spurring into a run, he shouted, "*El Gallo!*" and swung his rope as the horse swerved away from the thrusting pitchfork.

Rimbaud narrowly dodged the loop. He fended off Shafter's rope with the fork, ducked low as Booger Bill made his try, and stood there waiting while Jubal turned for another run. A hell of a way for a man to be taken, Rimbaud thought with self-accusing shame; like a dumb old mossy-horn backed up with its manure-scabbed rump against a slaughterhouse corral.

Three times they galloped past him, shouting and casting, and cursing their failure. Then, as Rimbaud fended off Jubal's fifth cast, he saw Booger Bill ride into the corral and understood that he would be outflanked here. Wanting a wall behind him, Rimbaud began a desperate march toward the cabin. And at this moment, as Jubal and Shafter came roaring at him, he remembered the Winchester. If he could reach that doorway, this game would be soon over!

Rimbaud ducked Shafter's loop. He dodged away from Jubal's long throw and now, as Booger Bill spurred in close, speared the big man's thigh with the sharp-tined fork. Bill yelped and yanked his horse into a pivoting turn that tangled the wasted loop. Rimbaud, hard pressed as he was, couldn't help grinning at the comical picture Booger Bill made. Spouting curses and tobacco juice, the big rider almost fell from the saddle attempting to extricate his fouled rope.

Diving warily away from Jubal's oncoming horse, Rimbaud made another zigzagging run toward the cabin. They knew what he was up to now and were confidently circling him, turning the yard into a dust-swirled ring. Red Shafter's next cast snagged the pitchfork. Rimbaud let it go, believing now that he would reach the cabin, exhilarated at the thought of turning the Winchester against these Roman Four raiders. By God, it would be a different tune then!

He was within ten feet of the doorway when a loop swished past his ears. He didn't know he was caught until the rope jolted him back and he was jerked down with an impact that knocked the wind out of him.

"*El Gallo!*" Hugh Jubal shouted triumphantly. "Hogtie him, Red!"

Dazed and gasping for breath, Rimbaud got to his knees. He tried to evade Shafter's grasping hands as the redhead swooped down on him with a pigging string between his teeth. But Jubal worked the rope expertly, keeping it taut so that the loop pinned Rimbaud's arms.

"You're a caught rooster," Shafter gloated. He tied Rimbaud's hands behind him, and now, as Jubal and Booger Bill got out of their saddles, Red asked, "What's next on the program, Hugh?"

"I guess we'll have a short intermission for supper," Jubal said. "Then there'll be en evenin' performance that'll be worth three times the price of admission."

Shafter laughed and said. "I admire shows that has freaks. You reckon there'll be a freak in this

109

one, Hugh?"

"Sure," Jubal promised. "The biggest goddam freak that ever come out of Mexico. You've heard of two-headed freaks, and them that has men's mustaches and women's tits. But this one is the best you ever saw—he ain't got no head at all. Just a little old bone knob sproutin' above his shoulders with no more brains than you'd find in the bottom of a parlor-house privy pot."

Loosing a hoot of ribald laughter, Red asked, "You mean it's alive?"

"Well, yes and no," Jubal said, giving this some thought. "It moves, and stinks, but it ain't got no sense or feelin'." He stepped around Rimbaud, who was still on his knees. "I'll help you up," he said mockingly, and knocked Rimbaud down with a boot in the back.

Dust got into Rimbaud's nose and mouth, choking him so that he gagged. He heard Jubal's cackling laughter, and felt a sickening sense of helplessness; of knowing he was to be maimed and could do nothing to protect himself.

"Now it's my turn," Booger Bill mumbled eagerly.

But Jubal said, "Not yet. We'd have no freak for our evenin' performance once you went to work on him. You got no restraint, Bill, no restraint at all."

Hugh stood there for a moment, idly kicking dust into Rimbaud's face, then ordered, "Go out back and keep watch for Maiben while Red cooks us some supper."

Tense with dread of being kicked in the face, Rimbaud kept his eyes closed against the gritty dust. There was a sadistic streak in Hugh Jubal that might prompt him to boot a man to death. The realization that this was so brought out a clammy sweat that drenched Rimbaud's taut body.

"You ain't the only one that's got a score agin him," Booger Bill objected crankily. "He busted my thumb, didn't he? And pistol-whipped me when I wasn't lookin'. That's more'n he done to you."

Jubal chuckled. "You'll git your chance," he promised. "You can give Rimbaud the finishin' touches."

"Finishin' is right," Red Shafter predicted.

Rimbaud listened to the receding footsteps as Booger Bill and Red moved off. Jubal remained, his boot propelling another spray of dust into Rimbaud's face. "You don't look so big, layin' down, and you don't talk so big," he jeered, the words merging into chuckling laughter.

He hawked and spat down into Rimbaud's face. "That's for me havin' to apologize on account of Lew's orders," he said, very calm and deliberate about this. "I sure wish the Shiloh crowd could see you now, with my spit on your cheek. I wish they could see the great Jim Rimbaud actin' tame as a whore's poodle."

Then his voice rose to a higher pitch as he ordered, "Git up on your knees, Rimbaud."

Rimbaud opened his eyes and blinked the dust out of them. It was almost dark now. A long shaft of lamplight came from the cabin doorway. Maneuvering himself to his knees, Rimbaud endeavored to get all the way up, but Jubal commanded, "Crawl to the house like the dirty stinkin' son you are! Crawl on your goddamn knees!"

Rimbaud peered up at him and asked flatly, "Afraid I'll be too big, standing up?"

Jubal snarled a curse. He kicked Rimbaud in the chest and knocked him down and shouted, "Do like I tell you, Rimbaud, before I kick your teeth out!"

CHAPTER ELEVEN

The cloudless, star-studded sky held a subdued glow but the earth was wrapped in a quilted shroud of darkness as Charley Bonn approached Boxed M balancing a fresh-baked apple pie on the pommel of his saddle. Even though Maria disliked having him ride at night, she was purely proud of her baking and wanted Jim Rimbaud to sample it. "The poor man probably didn't have a decent piece of pie all the time he was in Mexico," she'd said. "And I feel that we're beholden to him for standing up to Lew Stromberg like he did."

Jim Rimbaud, Charley reflected, had made a hit with Maria. Which seemed odd, her being so set on her husband acting peaceable and keeping out of trouble with Roman Four. Many the time she'd warned him to hold his tongue when Stromberg's riders poked fun at him. Yet she spoke of Rimbaud as if talking about a great white knight. Women, he guessed, were all mixed up in their minds.

There was a light in Maiben's cabin, and now, as Bonn was on the verge of announcing himself, he observed the vague shapes of horses standing in the yard. Two or three of them..

Charley pulled up at once. Those horses meant that Rimbaud had visitors; unwelcome visitors, most likely. Then, as he tallied three horses near the house and heard another moving over by the corral fence, the full significance of it burst on Charley Bonn: The riders of those horses were doubtless Roman Four men, and they were in the cabin—which must mean that Jim Rimbaud was either dead or disarmed!

That startling realization struck Bonn with the impact of a physical blow. If Roman Four could so swiftly eliminate Jim Rimbaud from the fight, what chances would lesser men have against Stromberg's bunch? He hadn't thought they'd even tackle Rimbaud. Not with his reputation. The man was supposed to be unbeatable with a gun, and wary as a wolf. How could they have outmaneuvered him so soon?

Easing his horse back into timber, Bonn halted and peered at the lamplit cabin. What, he wondered, had happened to Rimbaud? Was Jim dead, or disabled, or merely a prisoner? As always at times like this, Charley Bonn's strongest inclination was for flight. He preferred to play the cautious game, the safe game. But there was in him an inherent sense of loyalty that now held him. Because he had talked Rimbaud into guarding Boxed M, there was a responsibility here he couldn't ignore. And there was a prodding curiosity. What had happened to Rimbaud?

Yet even so, with this sense of loyalty and this curiosity in him, Charley was tempted to hightail it for home. Four horses meant four men. Tough, gun-toting men. It occurred to him that one of those horses might belong to Rimbaud; but even three Roman Four riders made the odds too high. He wondered if he could get to the cabin without attracting their attention. Perhaps, if he circled around afoot and came in from the back.

Dismounting, Charley placed the apple pie at the base of one tree and tied his horse to another. Then he drew his Winchester from the saddle scabbard, levered a shell into firing position, and walked slowly out of the trees. The rifle felt heavy in his hands. The weight of it reminded him that he had never shot at a human being. A man would probably get buck fever, aiming at another man for the first time. He'd probably miss by a mile.

Bonn had circled the cabin and was easing in toward an open kitchen window when he heard someone shout gleefully, "Pour it on him, Bill—Pour it on!"

Charley eased cautiously up to the peeled wall, hearing the meaty impact of fists against flesh, the scuff of feet, and gusty panting. What, he wondered, was going on? With a conflicting welter of apprehension and curiosity prodding him, Bonn cat-footed to the open window, peered along its edge, and was astonished by what he saw.

It was an odd sight. A grotesque yet curiously impelling sight. Jim Rimbaud, with his left hand tied down by a pigging string, and blood oozing from a gash on his forehead, slugged toe to toe with Booger Bill, who kept a bandaged hand off to one side as he swung with his right fist. Hugh Jubal stood near the kitchen doorway with a broad grin rutting his sorrel cheeks, while Red Shafter shouted, "Git him agin the wall, Booger. Crotch him!"

And now, as Rimbaud dodged away from Booger Bill's massive body, Shafter struck Rimbaud from behind.

Repelled by the brutal unfairness of it, yet fascinated by Jim Rimbaud's savage will to fight, Bonn watched in wide-eyed wonderment. There, by grab, was a fighting man—a real, go-to-hell fighting man!

It made Bonn proud to watch him. Proud and sad at the same time. Rimbaud was dazed and reeling on his feet, but he showed no sign of quitting. His blood-smeared fist swung like a

114

piston, pounding at Booger Bill's midriff, at his broad-jawed face and the bandaged hand. His lance-lean body was limber as a buggy whip; it arched forward each time he swung, then arched back to either side as he dodged Booger Bill's retaliating fist. But Jim was taking a terrible punishment despite his shifty weaving. The big rider caught him now with a solid smash to the face, that pulpy thud echoed by Jubal's hooting laughter.

"Bull's-eye!" the Roman Four ramrod shouted happily. "Slug him again in the same place!"

Rimbaud rolled with the punch, rocking back on his heels. Twin trickles of blood ran from his flared nostrils. He shook his head. He staggered sideways as if dazed, and Bonn thought: He's going down!

He dreaded what he would see when that happened.

But Rimbaud wheeled abruptly and targeted Bill's bandaged hand with a jab that brought a pain-spawned shriek from Booger Bill. The massive rider seemed to go beserk then. He bellowed obscenities the like of which Charley Bonn had never heard; dirty, foul-worded accusations about Rimbaud's parentage, vile references to his sexual relations with sheep. He barged at Rimbaud with the wild blindness of an enraged bull.

"I'll stomp your goddamn guts into the floor!" he shouted, tobacco juice dribbling nastily from the corners of his hate-twisted mouth. "I'll kick the manure out of you and rub your nose in it!"

He was like a man gone mad.

"You got to git him down first," Red Shafter scoffed. "Looks like I better help you."

But Jubal said, "Not yet, Red. Not yet. Give Bill another five minutes. He ain't doin' so bad, for a one-armed man who's a trifle touched in the head."

Charley gripped his Winchester in sweat-greased

115

hands, knowing he should use it now to halt this sadistic, one-sided deal. But even though he could get the drop on them, he wouldn't have the courage to shoot, and they'd know it. They'd know he was bluffing; would know he could no more shoot a man than he could strike a woman. Yet he couldn't just stand here and see Jim Rimbaud booted to death. That's what would happen when he went down, and with Shafter joining the fight, Jim would go down. He appeared wobbly on his feet right now,—as if his knees might buckle at any moment.

It occurred to Bonn that he could shoot out the lamp. That would end the fight, or at least give Rimbaud a breathing spell. But it would turn their attention to him, and he was afoot. A man wouldn't stand much chance with three of them gunning for him. Not on foot. He'd be shot down within ten minutes. But he had to do something, and do it quickly.

With that realization pounding in his mind, Bonn turned away from the window, walked out into the yard, and began running toward the trees where his horse was tied.

Jim Rimbaud rolled with punches he couldn't dodge. He gasped for air like a thirsty man gulping water. So much water he gagged on it. Blood ran into Rimbaud's right eye, blinding it, and blood was a warm wetness on his broken lips. He hit Booger Bill in the belly, and heard him grunt, and knew the big man was tired.

So am I, Rimbaud thought. So tired it took all his remaining strength to swing his fist. But he had to keep swinging; had to remain on his feet. If he went down now, with this wild bull of a man above him, he'd get kicked to death. He knuckled blood from his right eye and saw Booger Bill's fist coming at him, and attempted to dodge it. But the fist

116

smashed against the side of his head with an explosion that deafened him.

After that, for a time, Rimbaud was remotely aware of going down and getting up; of striking and being struck; of seeing Booger Bill's blurred, blood-smeared face wabbling queerly before him. There was no expression on Bill's face. It was blank, like a dead man's face. But his eyes weren't dead; they were wild and alive and red as the inflamed eyes of a mad bull.

Then, from nowhere at all, another face appeared—Shafter's narrow, grinning face—and he heard him shout, "Now you git it, Rimbaud! Now you really git it!"

Rimbaud remembered an old trick learned in a Sonora mescal joint. A risky, desperate trick used for survival. He went down sideways, landing on the palm of his free hand and kicking Shafter in the groin as the redhead lunged in. Shafter squalled a curse and grabbed himself at the crotch with both hands. Rimbaud got up, ducked Booger Bill's flailing fists, and knuckled blood from his right eye. He didn't see the fist that slugged him under the left ear. He tried to remain upright, but there was no strength in his legs. The floor tilted up and he heard Hugh Jubal brag, "That's how I chop 'em down—with one punch!"

Even then Rimbaud didn't go all the way down. He propped himself on his hand and was endeavoring to get up when Booger Bill kicked him in the side, again and again. And now, as sharp splinters of pain lanced along Rimbaud's ribs, he heard a gun blast, a deafening explosion echoed by a tinkle of shattered glass.

The kitchen went dark. There was the sound of a horse racing out of the yard, and Hugh Jubal shouting, "Come on, come on! That's Sam Maiben!"

After that, for a time, there was nothing at all.

CHAPTER TWELVE

Pain roused Jim Rimbaud, a sheath of pain that had its hot core in his left side. He put his hand there and felt no blood. He wondered about the pain, and the throbbing ache along his temples. And the darkness. Where the hell was he?

For a confused interval while clarity came by slow stages, Rimbaud lay rigidly braced against the continuing burden of his pain. Then he remembered being kicked. Booger Bill, he guessed morosely, had cracked his ribs. Or broken them. Recalling the gunshot that had smashed the lamp, and Jubal saying it was Sam Maiben, Rimbaud muttered, "That's what saved me."

But the Roman Four trio would be back. He attempted to untie his left hand, but the knot was pulled too tight. He hunched up on an elbow, cursed at the splinters of pain that movement brought, and waited while a wave of nausea washed through his sweat-drenched body. Then he tried to get his head around and down to the knot that thonged his hand to his left thigh, wanting to use his teeth on it. Again and again, while sickness gagged him, he endeavored to fight his way to the knot. But he couldn't quite make it.

And acrid odor of dust came to him. Listening intently, he heard the rumor of far-off hoofbeats, and thought: They're chasing Maiben. They would try to cut him off from Jigsaw Divide and turn him back this way. He wondered if the Winchester were still over there by the door. Taking a match from his pocket, Rimbaud thumbed it aflame and peered across the kitchen.

The Winchester was gone!

Rimbaud swore, knowing instinctively that Stromberg's men would return. Especially Booger Bill. The big man was loco with hate. Red would want another cut at him also in retaliation for that kick in the crotch. Those two would be back.

Remembering that Jubal had discarded his Buntline pistol in the yard, Rimbaud thought: I've got to get it before they return. With teeth clenched against the grinding pain in his side, he rose to his knees. A clutching weakness made him so dizzy that he had to support himself with one hand on the floor. The dark room seemed to be whirling around him in black, undulating waves. He waited for the dizziness to pass. But it got worse. He started creeping toward the door, and was sick. After that, for what seemed an endless nightmare of slow motion, he crept and rested and crept again, inch by pain-racked inch, while sweat coursed down his cheeks and the taste of it was salty on his lips.

Splintery pieces of the broken lamp globe cut the palm of his hand. It occurred to him that he should go around the glass fragments, but he was too tired, and there wasn't time for such maneuvering. He was sick again, and went into a long spasm of retching, and was so groggy he couldn't think straight. He saw that he was near the doorway, which seemed important. He couldn't remember the reason, or understand why he should be creeping on the floor like a drooling baby. A man should stand on his feet. Drunk or sober, a man should act like a man, not like a wet-diapered

119

baby. So thinking, Rimbaud reached for the doorframe to support himself, and missed it, and fell on his face.

Pain slashed his side with sharp claws. It brought a stark clarity to his mind, and in this moment of comprehension he heard the hoof tromp of a horse coming into the yard. One horse.

Booger Bill! Rimbaud thought instantly. Booger Bill coming back to stomp him!

But it might be Sam Maiben. Perhaps Sam had circled and come back to give him a hand. Then it occurred to Rimbaud that Maiben wouldn't do that. He'd know better than to lead those devils back here. So it must be Booger Bill riding into the yard.

Prodded by awful dread now, Rimbaud reached for the doorframe, grasped it, and tugged himself up. He had to get into the yard. Regardless of pain or dizziness he had to reach his gun, or be booted to death. Fighting to balance himself, Rimbaud staggered through the doorway, took one floundering step into the yard, and collapsed.

For a frantic moment, as he fought his way up out of the quilted blackness that engulfed him. Rimbaud thought he heard a voice that was far off, like the fragile echo of an echo. But it was too distant, and he wasn't sure he'd heard it, until Della Stromberg knelt beside him and asked urgently, "Did they shoot you?"

Even then Rimbaud thought he might be dreaming; might be imagining this. What would Della be doing here?

"Are you shot?" she insisted.

"No, but they booted my ribs," Rimbaud said.

"You poor man!" she cried. "Let me help you into the cabin."

"Find my gun first," Rimbaud suggested. "It's over there near the water trough. I'll need it when they come back."

"I heard the shooting," Della said worriedly, "and one rider going away fast. Was it Sam?"

"Reckon so."

"I hope they don't catch him," Della said. "Oh, I hope he gets away."

"How about getting my gun?" Rimbaud prompted. "I'm liable to need it any time."

It took a few moments for her to find it—moments while Jim Rimbaud listened for the sound of approaching riders. Long moments while his nerves drew wire-tight and he was like Sam Maiben had been this morning.

"A little more to the left," he directed impatiently when Della called for directions. And now it occurred to him that the Buntline might not be there at all. One of those bastards might have picked it up.

Again, as it had out here this afternoon, awful helplessness swept through him. He'd have no chance against them without a gun. And now, with a sickening sense of futility slogging through him, he heard Della exclaim, "Here it is! I've found it!"

"Good girl," Rimbaud said sighingly. "Good girl."

Afterward, when she'd given him his gun, Della went into the house and lit a lamp she found in the bedroom. Then she came out toting one of the drapes from a window, saying, "I'll bind your side with this."

Seeing the way perspiration greased his battered face as he sat up and took off his shirt, she said, "I wish there was some whisky for you. It might kill the hurt."

"There is," Rimbaud reported, and accomplished a grin. "On the bottom shelf, behind the flour and sugar."

And now, as he watched her go into the house, a sardonic sense of amusement came to him. What a joke this was—Lew Stromberg's daughter aiding the

121

man her father hated! And she was the girl he'd called a brat; the one he'd kissed with stud-horse passion the first time they met.

When Della fetched the jug, Rimbaud took a long swig, and sighed, and said gustily. "You're all right, kid. By God, you're plenty all right!"

That pleased Della and she showed it in the way she smiled at him. "You're all right yourself," she said, crouching down and getting her shoulder under his right arm. "I'll help you up."

It wasn't far to the four-poster bed. But it proved a slow and painful journey for Jim Rimbaud. Despite Della's supporting shoulder, he had to halt repeatedly, and each time she gave him a pull at the jug. When the last painful maneuver onto the bed had been accomplished, Della brought him a cup of hot coffee spiked with whisky, saying, "This will help you relax."

It did. The breath-taking barbs of pain lessened to a dull ache, and presently, as she washed his bloodstained face with a wet cloth, the ache dissolved into a wooden numbness. He had difficulty keeping his eyes open, especially the right one, which was badly swollen. He said censuringly, "You've got me drunk," and liked the sound of her girlish laughter.

"You remind me of Sam," she said, "because you're so helpless. He seems like that all the time. It makes me feel like doing for him."

Rimbaud felt sorry for her then, knowing how little chance there was of her winning Maiben away from Eve Odegarde. He wondered if Maiben appealed to Eve for the same reason. He said, "I guess you're not the only one who feels like doing for Sam."

"I guess not," Della agreed. A frown clouded her heart-shaped face and she said angrily, "But Eve Odegarde doesn't love Sam the way I do. You wouldn't catch her coming to him with food. He could starve to death in the brush for all she'd do. She's too much of a lady to traipse into the hills looking for her man when he's in trouble. But Sam doesn't seem to understand that. Sometimes I think he's stupid."

Stupid like a fox, Rimbaud thought. Maiben would take what Della had to give him, and then marry Eve Odegarde when he got in the clear. Nothing stupid about that.

So sleepy now that he could scarcely keep his eyes open, Rimbaud said, "Don't let me drowse off. No telling when those three sons will come back for another try at me."

"I'll take care of them," Della promised. "I can spook Booger Bill by just yelling scat at him. He's afraid of women."

She laughed.

It was an odd thing. The laughter seemed to merge with voices afterward, and Rimbaud thought he heard Della shout something to someone in the yard. One of the voices sounded like Hugh Jubal, which seemed important somehow. But he couldn't identify the reason. Vaguely, dreamily, he remembered being in a fight, but it was blurred and confusing, like a dream that didn't make sense. Once, when a sharp sliver of pain lanced his side, he heard Della's soothing voice and felt her soft woman's hand on his forehead. Her palm was astonishingly cool against his skin, which was peculiar, for they were sitting their horses in a switchback turn above Embrace Canyon and Della was perspiring as she told him about the singing laughter.

Or so it seemed. . . .

CHAPTER THIRTEEN

Eve Odegarde was in the kitchen, helping Limpy Smith with the breakfast dishes, when Mrs. Al Shumway came in and asked, "Can I see you alone for a moment, Eve? It's very important."

Mildly surprised, and wondering what prompted a social call this early in the day, Eve led her visitor out to the back stoop and closed the door. "Limpy won't eavesdrop," she assured Mrs. Shumway. "He has too many pots and pans to scour."

"Well, I certainly wouldn't want anyone to hear what I've got to say," Faith Shumway said, glancing nervously along the alley. "It's—well, downright personal, to say the least. And awful embarrassing."

This small, plump woman had a reputation for gossiping, and so Eve asked, "Are you sure you should tell me?"

Mrs. Shumway nodded, her pudgy face flushed and her eyes bright with excitement. "You're the one that's got to be told," she insisted. "I stayed awake half the night thinking about it, Eve. Thinking and asking myself whether I should be selfish and not tell you, or be a real Christian and do the difficult thing. I think we all have to face that question, at one time or another. It's what Reverend Pratt means when he preaches about us church members being inclined to follow the lines of least resistance instead of using our moral courage. Well, I don't suppose you'll like what I'm going to say, but I consider it's my Christian duty and I'm going to do it."

Eve smiled, thinking that more grief had been caused by gossips doing their Christian duty than by the sinners involved. "Does it concern Sam Maiben?" she asked intuitively.

Faith Shumway nodded, compressing her lips.

"And you think I should hear it?" Eve prompted.

Mrs. Shumway nodded again. "You're the only one that should know about it. The only one."

"Well, if it concerns Sam, I suppose it's all right for me to know," Eve said.

"It concerns him—and our Ruthy!" the woman announced with hissing insistence. "It's the most scandalous thing you ever heard tell of!"

Eve frowned and said, "You mean that Sam has—that he's involved somehow with your Ruthy?"

"Not just somehow," Faith Shumway hissed, "but like a man with a woman. Honey-fussin'— that's what he's up to, with our Ruthy that's scarcely more than a child. Al caught Ruthy with a man behind the corral last night about nine o'clock. They wasn't just standing there talking or holding hands."

Mrs. Shumway peered about, as if fearing someone else might be listening. Then she whispered, "They were on the ground, locked in each other's arms!"

Eve didn't say anything. She just stood there looking down, as if in deep thought.

"Well, the man rode off before Al could get a good look at him, but he suspicioned who it was, and when he asked Ruthy if it was Sam Maiben, she said yes," Faith Shumway explained. "Ain't that the most outrageous thing? Sam Maiben, with a posse chasing him and engaged to a fine girl like you, seducing our Ruthy with his slick talk and bold ways."

"But it couldn't have been Sam," Eve said quietly.

"You poor trusting girl, you," Mrs. Shumway sympathized, shaking her head. "I know how you must feel. As if somebody had slapped you in the face. I don't suppose it ever occurred to you that Sam Maiben might be a common scamp where women were concerned—a trifling, sneaky man betraying pure womanhood whenever he gets the chance."

"No," Eve murmured, "it never did." Then she asked, "What made your husband suspect it might be Sam?"

"Al knowed Sam had trifling ways because he's seen him with Della Stromberg on two or three occasions since Sam got engaged to you," Mrs. Shumway announced. She clucked and shook her head. "Imagine the shameful brass of him, messing with our Ruthy, and her just turned sixteen! He's a low, common scalawag, that's what he is!"

Eve remained silent for a moment revealing none of the shocked resentment that flared in her. Finally she said, "I wonder who Ruthy is protecting."

"What you mean—protecting?"

Eve shrugged. "It wasn't Sam your Ruthy was with last night," she said, with quiet confidence. "I'm certain of that."

"How so?" Mrs. Shumway demanded. "How could you be certain?"

"Sam rode into town at dusk yesterday," Eve

reported. "He had supper with me, then surrendered to Sheriff Robillarde. Sam was in Jail at nine o'clock."

"In jail!" Faith Shumway echoed.

Eve nodded, smiling a little at the woman's astonishment. "Perhaps it was one of the Isabelle boys who called on Ruth," she suggested.

"Oh, Lord—what've I done!" Mrs. Shumway wailed. "I shouldn't have told you!"

She grasped Eve's arm, pleading, "Promise you won't mention this to a soul. Not a single, solitary soul!"

"Of course I shan't," Eve agreed, "and you'd do well to forget that talk about Sam riding around with Della Stromberg. I happen to know the girl is infatuated with Sam, and has thrown herself at him on countless occasions, but it doesn't mean a thing. Sam can't keep her from riding with him if she insists. He's too much of a gentleman to be rude to her. As for him being a scamp with women, why, that's ridiculous, Faith. I'd trust Sam Maiben anywhere with anyone. He just isn't the trifling kind."

"Perhaps not," Mrs. Shumway admitted, too upset over her revealment of what had turned out to be a disgraceful family affair to argue about anything. "I'm sorry I said that about him, Eve—and I'm asking you again not to mention what I told you. I'll find out who the man was. I'll make Ruthy tell me. If he's fit for marriage, they'll be married quick. You can depend on that."

And at this moment Charley Bonn rode up the alley on a sweat-lathered horse. "Jim Rimbaud needs a doctor," he announced in a croaking voice. "I been trying to get here all night, but them Roman Four toughs kept cutting me off. By grab, it was awful!"

"What happened to Jim?" Eve asked, hastily stripping off her apron.

"Well, three of them ganged him in Maiben's cabin," Charley said, slumping in his saddle. "Booger Bill, Jubal, and Shafter. They slugged him considerable, all three of them. They had him down and Booger Bill was booting him to death when I shot out the lamp. Rimbaud may be dead by now."

"Oh, no!" Eve cried, and ran up the alley. When she passed the livery stable she called, "Harness Doc's horse, Joe, and please hurry!"

Ernie Link was sitting on the Alhambra Hotel veranda when he saw Eve Odegarde run toward Doc Featherstone's house. He was wondering about that as he watched Charley Bonn dismount in the livery-stable doorway. Something must be up.

Link took a short-snouted derringer from an inside pocket of his vest, using his left hand for this chore. He transferred the lethal little gun to his right hand, which was partially concealed by the bandaged cast that cased his broken arm from elbow to knuckles. Ernie had borrowed the derringer from Sheriff Robillarde's collection of captured weapons on the pretext of needing it to point at Sam Maiben in case the fugitive came to town. But Ernie had another reason for wanting a hideout gun. A more important reason.

Now, with his right hand hidden by the wide sling that supported the arm, Link went down the steps and crossed Main Street in time to intercept Charley Bonn.

"What you doin' in town so early?" Link inquired.

Charley shrugged and said evasively, "Might be come in for supplies."

"On horseback?" Ernie scoffed.

Bonn peered at him through bloodshot eyes. He said, "I don't reckon it's none of your business why I came in."

Surprised at such brashness from so meek a man, Link asked, "What you been drinkin', Charley? You must be drunk to talk like that."

"I been dodging my shadow long enough," Bonn said slowly, thinking this out as he went along. "A man can't side-step trouble all the time. He's got to take his share. It ain't no worse to be beat down, or even shot, than it is to be dodging all the time. A man gets tired of that. He feels sick to his stomach. Which is why I'm telling you it ain't none of your business why I came to town."

"Drunk," mused Ernie. "Drunk as a lord."

Then, as Bonn started to go past him, Link asked, "How do you like havin' Sam Maiben quit like a yeller dog?"

"What do you mean, quit?"

Link laughed and said sneeringly, "Why, Sam got a tight collar and gave hisself up last night, pretty as you please. He was so scairt he even had his lady friend walk to the jail with him, so's nobody would take a shot at him before he could ask Sol Robillarde to lock him up in a cell. I guess there never was a galoot more scairt than Sam Maiben. Nor so yeller."

Charley Bonn wasn't a man to curse. But he did now, exclaiming, "The damn fool! He'll go to Yuma sure!"

"Of course he will," Ernie agreed. "But maybe he's smart at that. Smarter than the rest of you nesters. He knows the Spanish Strip is open range and it'd take more than one Jim Rimbaud to keep Roman Four off it. Hell, I wouldn't be surprised to see Rimbaud come ridin' in any minute, now that

129

Maiben quit. The drifter can't draw wages from a man that's cooped up in Yuma Prison. So he'll quit too."

Then, seeing Doc Featherstone and Eve Odegarde hurry toward Gabbert's Livery, Link asked, "Where's Doc goin' in such a rush?"

Bonn didn't answer for a moment. Finally he said, "Might be Miz Swenson havin' another baby."

Whereupon he headed toward the jail to have a talk with Sam Maiben.

CHAPTER FOURTEEN

When Jim Rimbaud awoke it was coming day-light and Della stood by the bedroom window with his gun in her hand. He wondered why she should be holding a gun, and intended to ask her about the voices. But he drifted off to sleep, and when he opened his eyes again Della was beside him on the bed, her face so near he could feel the gentle brush of her measured breathing.

Lying motionless so as not to disturb her, Rimbaud wondered if his ribs were broken, or merely cracked. He took a deep breath, and feeling no pain, thought: Just sprung a trifle is all. He probed his side and found it so sensitive that he winced at the slight pressure of his fingers. He was aware of a soreness that sheathed his whole body; even his right hand was sore. Examining it, he grinned at sight of the bruised knuckles. Booger Bill would also have some sore spots this morning.

Rimbaud thought about last night—the half-remembered voices that had merged with his confused dreaming. Had he actually heard Hugh Jubal's voice, and if so, what had Della told her father's foreman? And what would he tell Lew Stromberg?

It occurred to Rimbaud that this impetuous girl sleeping so peacefully beside him had compromised herself in more ways than one by playing an angle-of-mercy role here. Contemplating her face now, with its relaxed features framed by dark, loosely tumbled curls, he remembered what she had said about being a rebel at heart. She was all of that, Rimbaud reflected; more of a rebel than Sam Maiben would ever be. And more honest about it. There was no false modesty in this girl, no pretense. She was prompted by strong impulses and the turbulent desires of a woman wanting a mate. Most folks seemed to think that decent women never felt an itch for a man; that only bawds and trollops got the mating urge. Such thinking, he believed, was counterfeit; like a lot of loco notions about women. Hell, they could have the same hungers and desires. They might hide the wanting a trifle, just to tease a man. But it was there, regardless.

Rimbaud looked at Della, understanding that she wanted Sam Maiben with a thrusting hunger, as he wanted Eve Odegarde. The fact that Sam happened to be her father's enemy made no difference to her. He could have been a bank robber or a murderer or a married man, and she would have loved him just the same. It was ironic, Rimbaud thought, that she should have fallen in love with a man who intended to marry the woman Lew wanted. An ironic and, for Della, a tragic thing.

Rimbaud didn't realize that he had dozed off until he heard a man announce, "Well, he's not dead."

Turning his head, Rimbaud saw Doc Featherstone. And then, as the medico leaned over to examine him, Rimbaud peered at Eve Odegarde, who stood in the bedroom doorway. There was an expression of shocked wonderment in her eyes, as if she was astonished at what she saw. Astonished and repelled. Rimbaud thought instantly: I must be a sorry sight. He grinned and said, "Good morning, Sweet Stuff."

"How do you feel?" Eve asked, not smiling.

"Like I'd been tromped by six shod broncs," Rimbaud admitted. "But I've felt worse and lived."

Doc Featherstone unwound the wide bandage and gave Rimbaud bruised flesh a squint-eyed appraisal. "Multiple contusions," he reflected, and watched Rimbaud's face for sign of pain as he probed the discolored rib section with gentle fingers. Seeing his patient's tight-clamped lips, the medico said, "Don't be too proud to wince. Relax, now, and let out a groan when it hurts."

Presently Doc said, "Two broken ribs. Perhaps three."

"You sure?" Rimbaud asked.

The medico nodded. "One more kick and you'd have had a punctured lung. In which case you'd have been dead by now."

Della sat up abruptly, yawned, and knuckled her sleep-swollen eyes. Then, seeing Eve in the doorway, she asked in astonishment, "What are you doing here?"

Eve shrugged and said, "I could ask the same question."

"Oh, you could, could you?" Della demanded angrily. "Well, if it's any of your business, I slept here. I spent the night with Jim Rimbaud and I don't care who knows it. Now what are you doing here, Miss Priss?"

Eve said quietly, "Charley Bonn didn't tell me there was someone to take care of Jim."

"Charley Bonn?" Rimbaud asked. "What would Bonn know about it?"

"He shot out the lamp here, and rode all night trying to get past Roman Four men," Eve explained. "Charley believed you were dying."

Rimbaud shook his head in puzzlement. "I

133

thought it was Sam Maiben who shot out the lamp," he muttered. "So did Hugh Jubal. Hugh said it was Sam."

"It couldn't have been," Eve said. "Sam gave himself up after supper last night."

Della got off the bed. "You mean Sam is in jail?"

"Yes," Eve said, adding tartly, "if it's any of your business."

Swift anger stained Della's cheeks. "So you talked him into quitting like a yellow coward!" she exclaimed. "You talked him into spending five years in Yuma just to spite me!"

Then, not taking time to tuck up her tumbled curls, Della shouldered past Eve and hurried outside.

Rimbaud heard her ride off while Doc Featherstone worked over him. Most girls, he reflected, would have been hugely embarrassed at being found asleep in bed with a man, even a wounded man. But not Della Stromberg. Rimbaud smiled, remembering how angrily she had accused Eve of influencing Sam Maiben. As if Eve had no rights in the matter at all. Lew Stromberg's daughter might be in disagreement with her father on many things, but she had inherited his temper and his arrogance.

"That girl is a case," Doc Featherstone said sighingly. "Never saw one like her."

"A good thing for me she's like she is," mused Rimbaud. "A proper girl wouldn't have been prowling around last night and found me."

Eve made no comment as she helped Doc with the final tight bandaging. She was, Rimbaud thought, as gracious as a woman could be; yet he sensed something in her eyes that was like disappointment, or a mild animosity, as if she resented the fact that Della Stromberg had spent the night here. But that didn't make sense. What difference would it make to her who slept with him?

Perhaps it was the fact they had occupied her bed, the big four-poster she'd given her husband-to-be. Women were odd about such things. She might even think the bed had been defiled.

Eve, who'd gone out to make a pot of coffee, came back into the room to announce that it was poured. Rimbaud saw her glance at the near empty jug. He smiled cynically, thinking that she would be mortified if she knew the jug belonged to her precious Sam. She probably wouldn't believe it if he told her, any more than she believed Sam was having an affair with Della Stromberg. Eve was that kind of woman. She would have faith in the man of her choice, no matter what anyone said about him.

"Try standing up," Doc Featherstone suggested.

Rimbaud eased off the bed. All his muscles ached, and soreness still sheathed his battered body, but there was no sharp pain as he took a few exploratory steps around the room. "Just like new," he announced.

Doc Featherstone sighed. "That's what the combination of youth and whang-leather toughness does for a man," he said crankily. "Beaten to a bloody pulp one day, on his feet the next. It's a crying shame that such resilience is showered on men who waste it so carelessly—who accomplish nothing worth while with it."

"You mean shiftless saddle tramps, don't you, Doc?" Rimbaud asked amusedly.

"I mean you," Featherstone said, and smiled in spite of himself. "It's envy, I suppose."

Afterward, when they'd had coffee and Doc was repacking his medical kit in the bedroom, Eve said, "You'd better come to town with us in the buggy, Jim."

135

"Why?" Rimbaud asked.

"Well, wouldn't it be much easier on you than riding horseback?"

"But I wasn't planning to go to town," Rimbaud said.

"You mean—you're not quitting?" Eve asked, her eyes wide with wonderment.

Rimbaud shook his head, whereupon a slow smile curved Eve's lips and fashioned tiny dimples in her cheeks. "You're an odd jigger, Jim," she said softly, as if thinking aloud. "You get drunk with dishwashers, and share whisky jugs with brazen flirts, and admit you're a shiftless saddle tramp. But you'll pay a debt to the last full measure, if it kills you."

Then she asked, "Aren't you jealous of Sam at all?"

"Sure," Rimbaud admitted frankly. "So jealous I'd like to see him spend the rest of his life in jail. But that doesn't change the fact that he once saved my life. A man can't forget a thing like that. Maiben going to jail didn't cancel out the debt, one way or another. And me not liking him doesn't change it, either."

"Sam took it for granted that you'd quit soon as you heard he had given himself up," Eve reported.

"But why should he?" Rimbaud asked, wholly puzzled.

"Well, you see, I told him how it was the night you came back," Eve admitted, a rose stain tinting her cheeks now. "It—well, it seemed only right that he should know."

"So your conscience was hurting you," Rimbaud suggested, a derisive smile rutting his bruised cheeks.

"No," Eve said, very sober and deliberate about this. "It wasn't my conscience that was hurting me, Jim. It was my heart."

And now, as Doc Featherstone came out with his black satchel, she whispered, "Be careful, Fiddlefoot."

The medico shook a finger at Rimbaud and said, "I don't want you to do any hard riding or lifting until those ribs have a chance to knit properly. And don't get into any fist fights. If one of those ribs punctures a lung, you're a gone goose, and being tough won't make a mite of difference. You'll die just as dead as a gentle Annie."

Rimbaud held up his right hand. "I promise," he said solemnly, and gave Eve a lingering appraisal as she got into the buggy. What, he wondered, had she meant about her heart hurting her? She waved to him and smiled as Doc drove out of the yard. He watched until the rig disappeared up the tree-bordered road toward Isabelle's Camp, hoping she would look back. But she didn't.

He went over to where the roan stood at the haystack and led it to the wagon shed. He daubed axle grease on its bullet-gouged rump, unsaddled it, and turned it into the corral. The brindle cow and calf were out of feed. He forked them some hay, and wondered again what Eve had meant. The thought came to him that she was the type of woman who would keep no secrets from her husband-to-be. The hurt she had mentioned was doubtless caused by her knowledge that Sam Maiben would be sent to Yuma Prison.

CHAPTER FIFTEEN

Rimbaud went into the house, took his gun off the bed, and examined its loads. Holstering the Buntline, he wondered how soon he would have to use it against Roman Four riders. They'd be after him in a day or two, he supposed; this evening, perhaps. Thinking how it had been yesterday, with Hugh Jubal kicking dirt into his face, Rimbaud muttered, "They won't catch me again.'

They might shoot him, but they'd never take him alive.

He cooked a meal, and ate it, and sat at the kitchen table for a long time, his ears alert to outside sounds while he thought about Eve. She seemed to accept the inevitability of Sam's conviction with the same composure she showed toward Limpy Smith's Saturday-night sprees. Eve had never been a talkative woman, or an easy-smiling one; but beneath the fragile shield of her pride was all the warmth and passion and receptiveness of ripe womanhood—a hidden treasure of love and affection waiting for a man who was doomed to prison. It hadn't occurred to Eve that there might be a way of saving Sam.

"Just one way," Rimbaud muttered.

He was thinking about that when the sound of a walking horse roused him to instant alertness. He drew his gun and stepped over to the doorway and could barely believe his eyes. For Lew Stromberg was riding into the yard. And he was alone.

It could be a trick, of course, Lew attracting his attention while others came up behind the barn or behind the wagon shed. But Rimbaud discarded that suspicion almost at once.

Halting his horse and raising his right hand palm forward, Stromberg called, "Is my daughter in that cabin?"

"No," Rimbaud said, keeping the Roman Four boss covered with his gun, and guessing why Stromberg had come alone. Lew wanted no witnesses to a scene that would have been hugely embarrassing to any father.

Stromberg peered at him in silence for a long moment, his black eyes squinted against the yard's bright sunlight. Finally he said, "Hugh Jubal says she was here after midnight, and run him off with a gun."

"So?" mused Rimbaud, understanding now that he hadn't dreamed about the voices. He knew also how great a debt he owed Della for driving off the Roman Four jackals. He flinched, thinking what would have happened if she hadn't been here to drive them off. With two ribs already broken, he would have been a sorry mess when they finished a second go at him.

Stromberg rode up to within a few feet of the stoop. He asked, "You sure she ain't here?"

When Rimbaud nodded, Lew asked, "When did she leave?"

Recognizing the trap in that question, Rimbaud said, "I didn't say she was here."

Stromberg glanced at the corral, then said, "I've got some news for you," and started to dismount.

"Wait until you're invited," Rimbaud said sharply. He stepped over to Stromberg and took his gun. Ejecting the loads, he returned it to Stromberg's

139

holster and said with mock politeness, "Light down, Lew, and rest your saddle."

"Thanks," Stromberg muttered. Seating himself on a corner of the stoop, he said, "Sheriff Robillarde brought me some news early this morning that I thought you'd be interested in hearing. Sam Maiben surrendered, and is in jail."

Rimbaud holstered his gun. He put his fingers to shaping a cigarette, and said quietly, "I guess Sam got sick of dodging. That's a sorry life, posse dodging. It addles a man's brain in time."

"Sure," Stromberg agreed. "Sam Maiben did the smart thing. No doubt about it. He's right where he belongs—in jail. And he'll be there for quite a spell, which means you're out of a job."

"Not exactly," Rimbaud said. "Of course, this isn't what you'd call much of a job, but such as it is, I've still got it."

"A jailbird can't pay wages," Stromberg insisted. "He won't even be able to buy your groceries. Be sensible, Rimbaud. You'd just waste your time staying here. And maybe get yourself shot in the bargain."

Stromberg plucked a cigar from his vest pocket and bit off its end. "I've got a much better proposition to offer you," he said. He took time to light the cigar and get it going, then added, "It's probably the best chance you ever had in your whole life."

"Had lots of chances," Rimbaud said, "and some of them were real good."

"Not like this one," Stromberg insisted. A smile creased his swarthy cheeks and he asked, "How would you like to marry my daughter?"

The unexpectedness of that question, and the bald confidence with which it was asked, astonished Jim Rimbaud. He took a deep drag on his cigarette; he exhaled the smoke slowly, and in this

140

interval of shocked silence Lew Stromberg said, "I know you ain't the marrying kind. You take what's handy and don't tie yourself down. But you'd be getting more than a wife in this deal, Rimbaud. A lot more. My girl must be loco about you, to do what Jubal says she did. Hugh couldn't understand it, but I can. It's the Spanish blood in Della. Romantic blood. Her mother was a Hidalgo, and Della is just like her. All heart and no head."

But even though that brash opinion might explain Della's rebel ways, it didn't make Stromberg's attitude seem reasonable to Rimbaud. The man had every right to detest him; to hate the drifter who'd made him back down in public. Yet Stromberg was suggesting marriage in the friendly fashion of a tolerant father eager to obtain a desirable husband for his daughter—a daughter he considered a trifle on the wayward side.

"What makes you so sure Della would marry me?" Rimbaud asked.

"Well, for one thing, she threatened to shoot Jubal if he didn't leave you alone," Stromberg said. "A girl wouldn't do that unless she was real high on a man. And she wouldn't have stayed here all night. Della is headstrong, and romantic like I said, but she's no blanket squaw taking up with any man that comes along. She's got a case on you, Rimbaud. That's plain enough."

It occurred to Rimbaud that Stromberg didn't know about Della's crush on Sam Maiben. Lew suspected she had been attracted to Maiben's hired hand, and had spent the past few evenings here. Lew had jumped at what seemed a logical conclusion. Rimbaud smiled, thinking how wrong Stromberg was, how little he knew about his own daughter.

"My son-in-law would automatically replace Jubal as ramrod," Stromberg announced, his voice taking on an emphatic tone of conviction. "With a man like you running the crew, Roman Four could spread out to its rightful size, whether Sol Robillarde goes to the legislature or not. And right now, the way the papers are pouring it on him, it don't look like he'll even be nominated. Sol's only chance against that Tombstone candidate was on a law-and-order campaign. Well, you busted that wide open when you shot Ernie Link and hoisted Jubal over the Shiloh bar."

"Too bad," Rimbaud said.

But that sarcasm was lost on Lew Stromberg. He said, "There's no reason on God's earth why Roman Four shouldn't be the biggest outfit on the border in time, perhaps the biggest in Arizona. It's just a case of spreading out—of taking what we want. A little at a time, of course, but taking it. And if Sol should happen to win out at the polls, we'd have him working for us in the territorial legislature, so there'd be no fencing of range between here and Tombstone. Not a goddamn strand of bob wire. Think of what that would mean to me—a hundred square miles of graze for Roman Four cows!"

Then Stromberg asked, "What you think of it, Rimbaud?"

Sparring for time to study this out, to identify the flaw in Stromberg's fantastic proposition, Rimbaud said amusedly, "It would be a good joke on Hugh Jubal, me being ramrod of Roman Four."

Stromberg laughed. It was a dry, rasping laugh without humor. "I guess you'd welcome the chance to put him in his place, after what he did here last night. Hugh was so full of brags he rode into town this morning for a little celebration."

"So?" Rimbaud said, and thought instantly: Then that's the place to catch him. In town.

"I've got the breeder stuff to stock a whopping

big range," Stromberg announced. "Good mother cows and some of the best bulls on the border. Real good blooded foundation stock. There ain't none better anywhere."

Then he asked, "Well, what do you think of my proposition?"

"I think it stinks," Rimbaud said bluntly.

Surprise propelled Stromberg into a spasmodic forward tilt. "You mean that?" he demanded. "You mean you don't want to marry my daughter—or be ramrod of Roman Four?"

And when Rimbaud nodded, Stromberg asked, "For God's sake, why not? What more could you want? What more could any drifter want than a pretty wife who'll one day inherit a big ranch? Have you thought of that, Rimbaud? It wouldn't be like you were risking your hide for somebody else just for wages. You'd be building something for yourself—a big future for your old age."

Rimbaud smiled thinly. "I told you once that I took after my drinking uncle who was partial to bourbon whisky and underdogs." he explained. "I'm not quitting Maiben."

"But he'll go to jail for three years," Stromberg protested, his voice high-pitched with bafflement. "He may even get five years. You planning to guard his place that long without pay?"

"Maybe yes, maybe no," Rimbaud said. "Hand me your gun, Lew."

Anger brightened Stromberg's black eyes. "You fool!" he raged. "You witless damn fool!"

Rimbaud drew his gun and triggered a quick shot so close to Stromberg's shoulder that he dodged instinctively. "Do like I say," Rimbaud commanded rankly, and when Stromberg handed over the empty gun he ordered, "Now go to the corral and saddle my horse for me."

That seemed to shock Lew Stromberg beyond

143

the power of speech or movement. It was, Rimbaud supposed, the first time this arrogant little man had ever been told to saddle a horse. The enormity of it drove the ruddy color from Stromberg's face, leaving his cheeks chalky.

"Do like I say," Rimbaud ordered, "and do it now."

Stromberg glanced at the gun. When Rimbaud's thumb drew the hammer back he walked across the yard in the reluctant fashion of a man doomed to irrevocable disgrace. And that, Rimbaud reflected, was what this amounted to for so proud a tyrant. Lew Stromberg had spent a lifetime ordering other man about. Now he was taking orders from a saddle tramp—from a fool who had refused to become his son-in-law. To Stromberg's way of thinking, he was being bossed by an idiot. It probably stuck in his craw so bad it choked him, Rimbaud thought. And he hoped it did.

Rimbaud dropped Stromberg's gun into the water trough. He watched Lew saddle the roan, checked the tightness of the cinch, and motioned for Stromberg to go to his own horse. He left the corral gate open so that the brindle cow could get at the haystack during his absence. It occurred to him now that he would probably never step foot in this yard again. Win or lose at Junction, he would be all through here.

A good place to be away from, he thought cynically. A place to forget.

There was only a slight discomfort as he climbed into the saddle; more of an abrupt ache than a pain. Doc Featherstone, he guessed, had done a good job of binding his broken ribs.

"We're heading toward town," Rimbaud said. "Mount up, Lew."

The ruddiness had returned to Stromberg's cheeks, but anger still gripped him. It showed in

144

the knotted tightness of his jaw muscles and the compressed thinness of his lips. He rode like a man in a daze, so clutched by the vicious intensity of his thinking that he was oblivious of movement, or the man who rode beside him, or the slope up which they rode.

When the trail narrowed Rimbaud ordered Stromberg to ride ahead, sensing that there might have been an intended double cross in Lew's nefarious bargaining. If there was to be an ambush, Roman Four's boss would be the first to face it. But Rimbaud was confident there would be none. Stromberg had meant what he said. All of it. The man had one monstrous ambition—to make Roman Four a big outfit. As Della had said, the ranch came first with him. Eve had sensed it also, understanding that the woman Stromberg married would play second fiddle to Roman Four.

Riding behind Stromberg now, Rimbaud wondered how any man could become so enslaved by an ambition; so warped by it that he would gladly promote the marriage of his daughter to a man whose gun might be beneficial to his lust for empire. It must be habit, Rimbaud thought; the accumulation of long years of stubborn endeavor. And of loneliness. Lew's wife had died young. Cheated of what had probably been his one grand passion, Stromberg had transferred his affection to the ranch—to improving and enlarging it, year after lonely year, until it had become an obsession that enslaved him.

And now, with his hope of having Sol Robillarde's legislative co-operation fading, with an offer to a saddle tramp flung back in his face, Lew Stromberg was like a groggy fighter.

Scanning the trail ahead with habitual wariness, Rimbaud followed Stromberg across Embrace Canyon and smiled at the memory of his first meeting with this man's daughter. Bare naked, he'd been, and hugely embarrassed. He chuckled, recalling how Della had struggled in an effort to evade his kiss; how hotly her temper had burned, and how quickly she had got over it. Little had he guessed then that he would one day owe her his life, or that the brazenness that had so angered him would be the basis for his survival. Fate, he reflected, played peculiar pranks on a man. Goddamn peculiar.

When they topped Big Mesa Rimbaud said, "Now you stay behind me, Lew, while I ride into town. I mean out of gun range."

"You planning to vent your spite on Hugh Jubal?" Stromberg asked, and when Rimbaud nodded, Stromberg warned, "Sol Robillarde won't stand for any more rough stuff in town. He'll throw you both in jail."

"Not me," Rimbaud said, and grinned, thinking how little chance there would ever be of Sol Robillarde's arresting him. Then he asked, "Did Shafter and Booger Bill ride into town too?"

Stromberg nodded.

So it's to be three against one again, Rimbaud thought, and rode on down the slope alone.

CHAPTER SIXTEEN

Dulcy Fay was in the tamarisk-shaded back yard, lolling comfortably on an old leather lounge, when Sheriff Sol Robillarde came around to the kitchen door. But Dulcy didn't see him, for she was absorbed in this week's edition of the *Tombstone Epitaph*. She was reading a story entitled: "Guns Blaze in Junction!"

Latest reports on Sheriff Sol Robillarde's alleged law and order campaign indicate that he is helpless to maintain the slightest semblance of either law or order in his home town of Junction. One man was critically wounded in one of three outbreaks of violence last Saturday night, and two other men were beaten to insensibility. One of the victims, a peaceable citizen named Severide, was pistol-whipped on Main Street in front of his horrified wife and two small children.

The shooting affray took place in the Shiloh Saloon when one Ernie Link allegedly, and for no apparent reason, began shooting at Jim Rimbaud. The latter, well known for his part in the recent Durango revolution, returned the fire and wounded his assailant.

According to reports, the Ladies Auxiliary of the Episcopal Church is up in arms because of what they term Sheriff Robillarde's lax and inadequate law enforcement. For the second time within a few weeks they have circulated petitions requesting his removal from office.

All of which makes it seem extremely doubtful that the harassed sheriff will be a candidate for the territorial legislature in the next election. In fact, it is reported by reliable sources that the powers that be have advised him not to run.

Dulcy was remotely aware of the voice of her cook saying, "Miz Fay is takin' her ease out back." But she didn't look up until Sol came over and said, "You look real comfortable with your shoes off."

She twiddled her toes and said pleasantly, "Take your boots off if you'd like, Sol."

"Can't, without a bootjack. They're not broke in yet."

Dulcy lowered the paper, not putting it aside. "Trifle hot to be gadding about in new boots," she suggested.

Robillarde took off his hat and mopped his perspiring forehead with a white handkerchief. "Never saw it so hot this time of year," he said as he sat down beside her on the lounge. "What's new in the paper?"

"Haven't you seen it?" Dulcy asked.

Robillarde shrugged. "Glanced at the front page, is all."

"It says here that you won't be a candidate for the legislature," Dulcy said. "Is that true, Sol?"

He nodded, and shrugged again, and said, "I guess there wouldn't be much chance of getting elected. I picked the wrong thing to campaign on—law and order. It seemed like a good issue last spring, because of all the trouble they were having at Tombstone, where my competitor comes from. But the darn thing boomeranged when things went haywire here."

Dulcy waited, as if expecting him to say more. When he didn't she said, "I'm truly sorry you won't get to be a big politician, Sol. You wanted it so bad."

"Just the way the cards fell," he said, making an open-palmed gesture with his smooth, uncalloused hands. "Perhaps it's all for the best. I like Quadrille Basin, and I'd hate to leave it. Especially Junction."

He smiled at her, and was reaching over to pat her shoulder when his eyes focused on an item on the back page of the paper. He stared at it, his smile slowly fading. He pulled back his hand and demanded, "Is that true, Dulcy—what it says there?"

"What?" she asked, turning the paper.

Then, as he pointed, she saw it; a paid notice that said in bold, black type:

WEDDING PLANNED

Miss Dulcy Fay will be united in matrimony with Patrick J. Finucane at a civil ceremony to be performed in Junction September 1st. A wedding supper, to be served at the Alhambra Hotel, will be attended by the couples' many friends in the southern Arizona town.

"Oh, that Finucane!" Dulcy exclaimed. "Isn't he the big push, now, putting that in the paper for everyone to see!"

"But is it true?" Robillarde demanded. "Have you promised to marry him?"

Dulcy nodded. "That I have," she murmured.

"Finucane says I should have a nice house of my own with just the two of us in it. And wasn't it sweet of him to have this put in the paper, just like I was some—well, some blushing bride in a white lace veil? He's the salt of the earth, that Finucane."

When she began reading the announcement aloud Sol Robillarde got up and put on his hat and walked out of the yard. But Dulcy didn't notice. She was pronouncing each word carefully, savoring its fine flavor.

CHAPTER SEVENTEEN

Circling north of the cattle pens, Rimbaud rode down a back alley to Gabbert's corral. Here he dismounted with deliberate slowness, guarding against strain to his bandaged ribs, and tied the roan. It had occurred to him that there was no way of telling exactly where Jubal would be, but because it was still a trifle early for supper, Rimbaud reasoned that Hugh would probably be at the Shiloh bar. So thinking, he walked toward the saloon's rear doorway.

A dust devil, twisting across vacant lots, swirled into the alley and ran along it, stirring tin cans to brief rattling. Rimbaud detoured around rubbish piles and swore softly as a black cat slunk across in front of him. Remembering that a similar cat had invaded Francisco Durango's camp shortly before the *federalistas* swooped down, Rimbaud thought: Just superstition. The black cat hadn't brought the federal hordes. A swivel-rumped woman had brought them, wanting a pouch of betrayer's gold to hide between her sweet-scented breasts. But even though he told himself that seeing a black cat now meant nothing, there was a sense of apprehension in him as he neared the Shiloh's back door. A man's reputation for fast, accurate shooting would stretch only so far, and there always came a time when it wasn't enough. A time when some bravo bastard got an itch to test it. If Jubal were alone there'd be no real trouble bluffing him down, for Hugh was a coward in his heart. But Red Shafter had a kill-crazy streak in him, and so did Booger Bill. Those two wouldn't bluff, which meant there'd be a shoot-out.

And now, as Rimbaud moved up to the open rear doorway, it occurred to him that he had nothing to win; that even if his desperate plan succeeded, he would collect only the privilege of riding out of Junction alone.

"A fool's privilege," he muttered.

With that conviction building a twin barrier with apprehension, Rimbaud halted abruptly. Why should he risk his hide to keep Sam Maiben out of prison?

Remembering the big four-poster bed, he thought: Why should I go out of my way to put them in it? For that was exactly what he'd be doing if he forced a confession from Hugh Jubal. He would be furnishing Sam Maiben a wedding night in the four-poster, with everything Eve had to give him. And she had plenty. Remembering how it had been the night she kissed him, with her woman's body arched against his body, Rimbaud swore softly.

There was a moment, with jealousy thrusting through him, when Jim Rimbaud teetered on the verge of turning back; when the risk seemed greater than his need of paying a debt "to the last full measure," as Eve had put it. A confused moment of indecision while emotion tugged him. While tension and resentment stormed through him, and subsided. While pride took over. The pride of a man who paid his debts.

Rimbaud shrugged, and stepped into the doorway, and peered at the bar, where several men stood drinking. This, he remembered, was where

Ernie Link had stood that time when a drunken dishwasher had spoiled his sly scheme. Rimbaud looked at the bar, thinking that this deal would be settled soon, one way or the other, if Hugh Jubal were there.

He was. Freshly shaved and wearing his Sunday shirt, Jubal lounged there with Red Shafter on one side of him and Booger Bill on the other. He was talking and smiling, gesturing with a hand that held a whisky glass. Shafter was smiling also, but Booger Bill just stood there, stolidly listening. A cynical smile quirked Rimbaud's lips at the knowledge that this would be three to one—the usual odds for a Sonora Serenade, he reflected as he walked on into the saloon. He was within fifteen feet of the bar when Hugh Jubal swung around and stared at him.

"You!" Jubal blurted in a queerly croaking voice. "What you doin' here?"

"Hunting skunks," Rimbaud said. "Three stinking skunks."

He made a tall and menacing shape standing there with his right hand hovering close to his holster; a dark, poised shape that prompted men to move hastily away, leaving Roman Four in exclusive possession of the bar. Even Pat Finucane took one look and then ducked around the front elbow to join a group against the side wall. It was that plain.

All this in the moment before Rimbaud announced rashly, "You're first, Red. See if you can break my arm like you bragged yesterday."

Shafter's eyes tightened. "Sure," he said, a brassy smile creasing his cheeks. "Sure. But it won't be your arm, Rimbaud."

Hugh Jubal sidled away from Shafter and bumped into Booger Bill. He backed up a step and said crankily, "You only got what was comin' to you. No need to start a shootin' scrape on account

153

of a thing like that."

"It's running out of your donkey ears," Rimbaud said.

"What is?"

"The yellow. That dirty yellow they call coward juice. But from now on they'll call it Jubal juice around here. They'll remember how it ran out of your big donkey ears."

Even though he spoke to Hugh it was Red Shafter that Rimbaud was narrowly watching. For Shafter would make the first move, Rimbaud was sure, and now he thought: Booger Bill will be a close second. Jubal might act, or he might not, depending on how the play went; how high the odds were in his favor.

Shafter stood tensely poised, his body slightly arched so that his shoulders were tipped forward. Rimbaud saw the wicked flame that flared up in his eyes a split second before Red's splayed fingers grasped the ivory grips of his gun. And at this instant, as Rimbaud drew and fired with one swift smooth-flowing motion, Booger Bill's hand made a white blur above his holster.

Rimbaud slammed two bullets into Shafter's shirt pocket and then fired at Booger Bill, those three shots coming in such rapid succession that the reports merged into one long roar of room-trapped sound. Red Shafter's gun exploded as he collapsed, the bullet splintering a floor board six inches in front of Rimbaud's boots. But Booger Bill's clumsy draw hadn't been completed as he fell back against Hugh Jubal, who now jerked aside with both hands held shoulder high.

"Don't shoot!" the Roman Four ramrod yelled shrilly. "I ain't drawin'!"

Even though Rimbaud had counted on this, knowing it was his only chance for success, Jubal's cowardly surrender angered him. "You dog!" he scoffed. "You stinking yellow dog!"

Booger Bill, with blood staining his shirt, had propped himself on hands and knees. Now he reared back and tugged his gun from the holster with both hands. Rimbaud cursed, and fired, and watched the big man tip over in the slow ponderous way of a sledged bull going down.

"Dead," Hugh Jubal muttered, staring at his two sprawled companions. "They're both dead."

And over by the wall Joe Gabbert blurted. "They should've knowed better than to draw agin him."

Rimbaud was remotely aware of voices out in the street, and now, as he holstered his gun, faces appeared above the batwings. But his chief interest was in the frightened man who stood in front of him; the gawking coward he had come here to catch. He peered at Jubal now and said sharply, "Your turn, Hugh."

Perspiration greased Jubal's fear-chalked cheeks and made a glistening necklace around his wattled throat. "I ain't drawin'," he announced sullenly. "It would be suicide."

Rimbaud laughed at him; harsh, hooting laughter that sounded loud against the saloon's strict silence. "So you want it cold turkey," he jeered.

"No!" Jubal protested. "By God, you can't do that!"

"Who'll stop me?" Rimbaud asked, knowing this was the acid test of all his planning; the test that would mean the difference between freedom or prison for Sam Maiben.

Jubal glanced at the group of silently watchful men along the side wall as if pleading for help. His right hand made a habitual gesture toward the Durham sack in his shirt pocket, then came away, and he said again, "It would be suicide."

Sheriff Sol Robillarde stepped through the

batwings, demanding, "What's up? What's up?"

"You keep out of this," Rimbaud commanded, not shifting his gaze from Jubal's fear-blanched face.

"But I'm the law here," Robillarde protested.

"You won't be, Sol, if you mix in this," Rimbaud told him flatly. "You'll be dead as a ruptured duck."

Then he said to Jubal, "How about it, Hugh?"

Dread was a plain and shameful thing in Jubal's eyes. He had lowered his hands but now kept the right one well away from his holster. "You can't just shoot me down like a—a dog," he insisted.

"Oh, yes I can," Rimbaud corrected. Then he said savagely, "You're going to get it, Hugh—unless you talk."

"Talk how?"

"Talk straight and fast."

Jubal blinked his eyes and said, "I don't know what you mean."

"You know, all right, and you've got just one minute to get it told, out loud, so everyone can hear you."

Jubal shook his head. "I don't know what you mean," he whined.

It occurred to Rimbaud now that perhaps he didn't; that Sam Maiben might have lied about not changing the Roman Four brand into a Boxed M. In which case Jubal *wouldn't* know what he was talking about. That possibility ripped at him with sharp claws. This would be a sorry spectacle if Sam had lied; a God-awful spectacle.

But his frowning face revealed none of this doubt as he said, "I always did hate a liar, Jubal. And you're the biggest goddamn liar I ever met." Then he snarled, "Talk, Jubal—or take it in the gut!"

Hugh held out both hands, palms forward, as if

to shield his body. "You mean about that Roman Four brand that was worked into a Boxed M?" he asked croakingly.

Rimbaud nodded, only the brighter shine of his eyes showing the exultation that rifled through him as Jubal muttered, "Well, I done it. The boss threatened to fire me if I didn't git the goods on Maiben. Lew suspicioned Sam was stealin' calves, but we couldn't never catch him at it."

"Did you tell Stromberg how you framed Maiben?" Rimbaud asked.

Jubal shook his head. "I just done it to save my job."

Rimbaud glanced at Sol Robillarde and asked, "Is that enough confession to turn Maiben loose, or do you want it in writing?"

"It's enough," Robillarde said. He glanced at the two bodies and sighed, saying, "Enough to knock my political career in the head too." Then he looked at Jubal and said, "I guess you better come with me, Hugh."

Jubal shrugged. He turned and followed Robillarde in the dazed fashion of a man walking in his sleep.

Doc Featherstone bustled in with his little black bag. He examined the bodies, then peered curiously at Rimbaud, "You shoot real straight for a man with two broken ribs," he said frowningly.

Rimbaud grinned. "You tied 'em up real nice and tight, Doc. I'll stop by and pay you before I pull out."

"You leaving Quadrille Basin?" Featherstone asked.

Rimbaud nodded, and was turning toward the batwings when Lew Stromberg elbowed his way through the crowd. Roman Four's boss flicked a glance at the sprawled shapes of his dead riders, then looked at Rimbaud and exclaimed, "You

157

work fast, Rimbaud! Awful fast!"

Again, as he had one other time in this room, Rimbaud asked, "Any objections?" and glimpsed Della Stromberg's face in the doorway throng.

"Yes, by God!" Stromberg announced in a rage-clotted voice. "Objections aplenty!"

There was no indecision in him now. No sly caution spawned by his greed for graze. Raw red temper blazed in Stromberg's eyes as he sprang forward, leaned over, and reached for the gun in Red Shafter's rigid right hand.

Instinctively, without conscious thought or volition, Rimbaud made his draw, and heard Pat Finucane shout, "No, Lew—no!"

In this tumultuous moment, as Della Stromberg screamed and darted toward her father, Jim Rimbaud remembered that he owed another debt—an angel-of-mercy debt that needed paying here and now. No matter what it cost.

With that monstrous conviction pounding through him, Rimbaud stood there unmoving as Stromberg wrenched the gun from the death grip of Shafter's fingers; watched the barrel swing up, and saw Della grasp her father's arm as the gun exploded. That bullet ripped splinters from the bar beside Rimbaud, and it was echoed by Della' hysterical command, "Drop it, Dad! Drop it before he kills you!"

Obediently, as if impelled by a will stronger than his own, Lew Stromberg dropped the gun. It was an odd thing. All the anger faded from his eyes; there was a meekness in them and a bafflement. Della clung to him, softly sobbing. He placed an arm around her shoulders and said, "Hush, child. I'm all right."

Then he looked at Rimbaud and said wonderingly, "You could've shot me. But you didn't. Why?"

158

Rimbaud shrugged, marveling at the abrupt admiration he felt for this little man. Lew Stromberg was now as he'd always been, Rimbaud supposed: greedy and arrogant and cautiously conniving. Even though there was a meekness in his eyes and in his voice at this moment, he was probably no different than before. But he wasn't a coward. Lew had proved that when he reached for Shafter's gun. And he was man enough to admit publicly that he'd made a monstrous mistake—that only another man's decision not to shoot had saved his life.

"Why didn't you shoot?" Stromberg demanded.

"Ask your daughter," suggested Rimbaud.

"But I thought you said you didn't want—"

Rimbaud cut him off, saying, "You think too much and you talk too much." He wanted no reference to the marriage proposition here.

Stromberg continued to stare at him, as if unable to believe that so notorious a gunman had refrained from shooting. He said, "I'm much obliged, Rimbaud. Real obliged."

"Enough to do me a favor?" Rimbaud asked slyly.

And when Stromberg nodded, Rimbaud said, "Leave those Spanish Strip folks alone."

"I will," Stromberg agreed. Then a self-mocking smile creased his dark face and he added, "After what's happened I ain't got much choice."

Rimbaud liked that. He said, "That's fine, Lew."

Observing that the crowd outside was so large it bulged through the batwings, Rimbaud walked to the rear doorway and was stepping into the alley when Limpy Smith called, "Wait up, Jim! Wait for me!"

Rimbaud frowned, wanting to be alone; wanting to relax and let the tension run out of him. "I'll see you later," he said.

But the little dishwasher hurried out, his peg leg creaking and his bald head glistening with perspiration. "I owe you a drink," he announced jubilantly. "By grab, we got to celebrate, friend Jim. We just got to!"

Rimbaud felt like protesting that he had nothing to celebrate; that he'd won nothing here except the slogging sense of futility that always crawled through him after a shoot-out. A cold and clutching futility that whisky couldn't kill. But Smith's friendly eagerness made Rimbaud discard a blunt rejection, and so he said, "Later on, Limpy, when things quiet down a bit."

"I'll be through work at eight o'clock," Smith said, so excited by what he had seen that he couldn't stand still. "You be here at eight o'clock and we'll have us a hell-smear of drinks. Just like that other night."

Rimbaud nodded and went on along the dusk-veiled alley. Recalling the black cat that had crossed his path, he mused, "Didn't mean a thing." But even though his plan had worked out perfectly, there was no satisfaction in him. He had paid a debt this afternoon; an obligation that had begun with a bullet fired on the far-off Ruidoso. And that debt had spawned another, which he had also paid. Remembering other times he had felt like this, Rimbaud swore morosely. There would be more of them. No matter where he went, it would always be the same. Other debts and other payments.

Slowly, in the plodding way of a man bone-weary, Rimbaud walked back to his horse. And presently, leading it past the back stoop of Eve Odegarde's restaurant, he looked at the kitchen hoping for sight of her. But the kitchen was empty, and he thought: She'll be welcoming Sam Maiben out of jail. Eve was probably kissing him now;

giving him a taste of all the wild sweet flavor that was in store for him. Rimbaud grinned, glad that he had taken one taste himself. Remembering how passionately Eve had responded, he said to himself, "That's one kiss Sam Maiben will never get."

Whereupon he led his horse into the deserted stable and unsaddled it.

CHAPTER EIGHTEEN

Ernie Link had been visiting a girl friend on Residential Avenue when the shooting started at the Shiloh. He ran most of the way, but it was all over by the time he got there. A crowd milled about in front of the saloon, morbidly watching Coroner Green and his son tote out the bodies of Booger Bill and Red Shafter.

"What in hell happened?" Ernie asked a bystander.

"Jim Rimbaud killed hisself a couple more men," the fellow reported. "He's a ring-tailed heller, that Rimbaud."

Cautiously protecting his sling-supported arm, Link pushed through the crowd to where Joe Gabbert stood on the saloon stoop relating his eyewitness version of the fight. "You never seen nothin' like it," Joe announced dramatically. "There was Red and Booger Bill both grabbin' for their guns. Both of them, mind you. It looked like Rimbaud didn't have a chance. But he shot 'em down quick as a flash—one, two, just like that. He put a pair of slugs into Red's shirt pocket slick as a man shootin' at a target. You could cover both them bullet holes with a silver dollar, they was that close together. Them two slugs killed Red instantly. He was dead before he ever finished drawin' his gun."

"How about Booger Bill?" a man inquired. "What was he doin' all this time?"

"Time nothin'," Gabbert scoffed. "Hell, there wasn't a split second scarcely between them two shots at Shafter until Rimbaud turned his gun on Booger Bill and slammed a bullet into him quick as the dart of a toad's tongue. They had him three to one, but Hugh Jubal never even grabbed. He just lifted his paws and howled for mercy. It was the damnedest thing you ever saw."

Al Shumway, who'd just driven into town with his family, asked, "Is Rimbaud still in there?"

"No," Gabbert said. "He went out the back way soon as it was finished." Then Joe added laughingly, "This puts the finishin' touches on Sol Robillarde's chance of goin' to Prescott. He said as much himself. That Tombstone man will win hands down for sure now."

Ernie peered along the darkening street and identified Buck Aubrey standing at the corner of a cross street with a girl. Walking over there, Link said, "You seen Rimbaud since the fight?"

Buck shook his head. "I was in the barbershop gittin' a haircut when it happened," he said. "Never did git to see Rimbaud, and don't have no hankerin' to. After what he done to Booger Bill and Red, I don't ever want to see him."

Ernie peered at the girl and asked, "Ain't you Al Shumway's daughter?"

She nodded, and now Buck said, "Me and Ruthy are gittin' married this evenin' at eight o'clock."

"Married!" Ernie blurted. "To a Spanish Strip girl?"

And when Buck nodded, Link said, "Lew'll fire you sure as hell. He won't stand for any man of his marryin' into a homestead family. He'll fire you sure."

"Shouldn't wonder," Buck admitted. "But I'm

163

doin' it regardless. There's other cow outfits where a man can work. Plenty of 'em if a man goes far enough. Quadrille Basin ain't the only place in the world."

Link shook his head. "You don't know when you're well off," he said. "Wait till you been married a while and it wears off. You'll git tired of sleepin' with the same woman every night, week in and week out, month after month. I tried it once and it was awful. You'll wish you'd kept away from preachers."

"I think you're fresh!" Ruthy exclaimed, taking Buck's arm and leading him away from Ernie. As they crossed the street, she asked, "It won't wear off for us, will it, Buck?"

"Never," Buck said, squeezing her arm. "Not in a hundred years."

Ernie turned back to the crowd in front of the Shiloh and listened to the talk. Folks were all worked up about the shooting; they kept wagging their jaws about it, like it was the biggest thing that had ever happened in Junction. Bigger, even, than the night Rimbaud had shot him. There'd been considerable excitement then, but not like this.

"Three to one they had him," a man exclaimed, "but Rimbaud was too fast for 'em!"

And another man said, "Jim Rimbaud is the fastest gun-slinger in the country, bar none. He'd make Wyatt Earp and Doc Holliday look slower'n sorghum in January. Why, you can't even see his draw, it's that fast."

Jim Rimbaud. His name was on every tongue. Jim Rimbaud this, Jim Rimbaud that. It made Ernie squirm with envy each time he heard it. That's the way folks would have talked about him if he'd had a little luck with that first shot in the Shiloh. They'd have talked about Ernie Link, and told how he chopped down Jim Rimbaud. It was a crying shame the way he'd missed his chance that night. And he'd missed by so little; probably not more than an inch or two. But instead of hitting Rimbaud, the bullet had merely broken a front window, and so nobody had talked about Ernie Link. They'd just wagged their goddamn jaws about Rimbaud. Like now.

Link drifted over to the Alhambra lobby and glanced at the register. It was there, big as brass: "Jim Rimbaud, Two Tanks, Texas. Room Number 9."

Who'd ever heard of Two Tanks, Texas? Must be some little old cow town in the brush. No one had heard of Two Tanks. But everyone had heard about Jim Rimbaud. He was better known than the town he came from. That showed what a gun reputation could do for a man. It could make him bigger than a town.

Ernie went out to the veranda and surreptitiously transferred the little double-barreled derringer to his right hand. The man who gunned down Rimbaud would be famous. He's be better known than Junction, Arizona.

Ernie grinned, visualizing how it would be, with folks gawking at him, and pretty girls saying how brave he was to go against Rimbaud with a broken arm. Hell, he'd be a regular brass-riveted hero and have his pick of girls.

CHAPTER NINETEEN

Jim Rimbaud was on the bed half asleep, when someone knocked at the door of his hotel room. He had left the bracket lamp burning and now reached for the holstered gun he had draped over a bedpost. Who, he wondered, would be calling on him? Not Sheriff Robillarde, surely. Sol wouldn't have the brass to try holding him for an inquest. It might be Limpy, or even Della Stromberg wanting sympathy after seeing Eve welcome Maiben out of jail. Well, he could give her that; but damned little else. He felt all washed out; empty as a discarded bottle.

The knock came again.

"Who's there?" Rimbaud called, feeling no sense of apprehension; feeling nothing beyond a languid, benumbing weariness.

"Me—Sam Maiben."

"Come on in," Rimbaud invited, and was holstering his gun when the door opened.

Maiben came over to the bed and shook hands in the queerly solemn fashion of a man going through a necessary ritual. "I'm sure much obliged," he said soberly. "You took long chances tackling Jubal and those others like you did. Awful long chances."

Then, frankly curious, he added, "I don't see how you done it, or why."

·Rimbaud shrugged, still resenting this man who would be Eve Odegarde's husband, and embarrassed by his gratitude. Why did the damn fool have to stand around and talk? He had fulfilled his social obligation, probably at Eve's suggestion, so why in hell didn't he hightail back to her now?

As if sharing a kindred embarrassment, Maiben said, "Well, things have sure changed considerable since the last time we met, Jim. For me and some others. I never saw the beat of it. You wouldn't think so much could happen in so short a time. Take Lew Stromberg, for instance. He don't act like the same man."

Maiben walked over to the doorway and turned, and said in an odd, flat voice, "Eve told me to tell you it's not too late for supper if you'll eat in the kitchen."

Then he went out and closed the door.

Rimbaud smiled, recalling how Eve had told him that once before. This invitation, he supposed, was her way of thanking him for clearing Sam; for furnishing them a marriage bed. She would have a new name soon. Eve Maiben. Mrs. Sam Maiben. But she'd always be Eve Odegarde to him.

"Well," mused Rimbaud, "I can stand some food. And I might get a farewell kiss for dessert."

It was odd how the memory of one kiss could devil a man; how the remembered pressure of one pair of lips could make a man forget every other woman he had ever known. Rimbaud buckled on his gun belt and went downstairs, noticing that it was ten minutes to nine by the lobby clock. He grinned, guessing that Limpy Smith was waiting for him at the Shiloh and probably half drunk already. He was a great one, that Limpy; all he wanted from life was a little sociability and a chance to brag about Doc Odegarde. Life could be a lonely thing without companionship.

167

Rimbaud was going down the veranda steps when he saw Smith coming across Main Street with a quart bottle in his hand. And at this same instant, as the dishwasher called, "I brung some celebration," Rimbaud observed Ernie Link lounging against the hotel hitch rack.

"I got somethin' to tell you," Link announced.

The tense tone of his voice stirred a faint bell of warning in Rimbaud's brain, yet the doorway's shaft of lamplight revealed no gun at Ernie's hip.

"Save it for some other time," Rimbaud suggested.

Limpy, thinking this was meant for him, protested, "But we was goin' to celebrate tonight."

"Smith, you stay right where you're at," Link ordered, not turning to look at Limpy. And now, moving his sling-supported right arm a trifle, he shouted angrily, "Draw, Rimbaud! Draw your gun!"

Utterly astonished by that challenge, Rimbaud stared at Link in disbelief. "You gone loco?" he demanded.

"What's loco about me and you settlin' our grudge?" Ernie scoffed. "You had the luck before. Mebbe I'll have it this time."

And then, as Ernie's right arm moved again, Rimbaud saw the twin snouts of the derringer, and understood that he was looking into double-barreled death.

"A cold deck," Rimbaud muttered, calculating the distance between them at less than fifteen feet and knowing it wasn't enough. If he dropped flat the first bullet might miss him, but not the second one.

"I'm givin' you a chance to brag," Link taunted. "The same chance you gave Red and Booger Bill."

Rimbaud laughed at him. "Did you say chance?" he asked.

168

But there was no mirth in his laughter. This, he understood, was the thing he'd known would happen to him someday. It was inevitable. He had expected it, yet now that he was seeing it, and feeling it, he couldn't quite comprehend why Ernie Link was so set on killing him. The feud between Roman Four and the Spanish Strip homesteaders was over.

"What you waitin' for?" Link called scoffingly. Then his voice rose to high-pitched shrillness as he yelled, "Right now, Rimbaud! Grab right now!"

Rimbaud went down sideways with the derringer's report like the crack of a buggy whip above his head, that sound echoed by a crash of breaking glass. Rimbaud snatched up his gun, but he didn't fire it. He just lay there, propped on the palm of his left hand, and peered at Ernie Link, who was draped head-down across the hitch rack.

It was the most astounding sight Jim Rimbaud had ever seen. The most unexpected and inexplicable. For he hadn't fired a shot.

Rimbaud got to his feet, wholly confused, and looked at Limpy Smith, who stood behind the hitch rack with the neck of a broken bottle gripped in his hand.

"Colonel's Monogram," Limpy muttered, peering at the whisky that dripped from Link's dangling head.

That was when Sheriff Robillarde came running up, and glanced at Link, and said wearily, "Another corpse for Art Green."

"No, just a drunk," Rimbaud corrected. "Ernie took a whole quart of Colonel's Monogram at one gulp."

And then, seeing the disgusted expression on Limpy Smith's face, Rimbaud loosed a whoop of rollicking laughter that hurt his side.

"What's so comical about me losin' a quart of

good bourbon?" Smith demanded.

Rimbaud walked over to him. "You did it again, by God—you did it again," he said, and patted Limpy's shoulder with real affection. "You saved my bacon for the second time, *amigo*."

Then Rimbaud dug a gold piece from his pocket, saying, "Go buy another bottle, Limpy. I'll be over after I eat some supper and we'll have us a grand celebration. If Pat Finucane so much as frowns at you, tell the monkey-faced Mick I'll shoot his goddamn ears off."

Still chuckling, Rimbaud turned and was crossing Main Street's wide pattern of alternate light and shadow when Eve Odegarde rushed up to him.

"Are you all right?" she demanded. "I heard a shot."

Her cheeks, faintly revealed by reflected lamplight, were flushed and marked by the sooty shadows of her long lashes. Rimbaud grinned, his eyes frankly appraising. "You shouldn't be worrying about shiftless saddle tramps," he chided. "What will Sam Maiben think?"

"He knows," Eve said quietly.

"Knows what?"

"Well, how it is with us."

And then she held up her left hand, showing him that the ring was gone. "I couldn't quit Sam while he was in trouble," she explained, her subdued voice barely above a whisper. "And there seemed no way to get him out of it. I—I just couldn't quit him when everything was bad for him, Jim."

"You couldn't?" Rimbaud echoed dully.

"Don't you see how it was, Jim, with a posse chasing him and all? There didn't seem to be a chance of his being acquitted. I wanted to tell you how it was, that first night after you kissed me. But I couldn't think up the right words, or trust myself to be near you."

Slowly, in the deliberate way of a man not sure of his senses, Rimbaud reached over and tilted her face so that he could see into her eyes. For a long moment he looked into them, not speaking or smiling. Just looking. And seeing all a man would ever want to see in a woman's eyes. Then he asked, "Is that what you meant, when you said your heart was hurting you?"

Eve nodded, meeting his gaze fully, as if willing for him to see how it was with her; wanting him to see.

"You did two women a favor when you cleared Sam of the rustling charge," she said. "Me and Della Stromberg. Della's been chasing Sam for months. Now she's got him."

"And I've got you," Rimbaud said, taking her in his arms.

Her lips were there for him, moist and gently smiling; and her eyes, so warmly glowing, held a frank eagerness that hugely roused him. Yet he waited, savoring her womanly fragrance, and said, "Sweet Stuff," in a more humble tone than he'd ever used. Then he kissed her, and felt the full, sweet pressure of her lips, and knew there'd be no more lonely trails for him, ever.

Leslie Ernenwein was born in Oneida, New York. He began his newspaper career as a telegraph editor, but at eighteen went West where he rambled from Montana to Mexico, working as a cowboy and then as a freelance writer. In the mid 1930s he went back East to work for the *Schenectady Sun*. In 1938 he got a reporting position with the *Tucson Daily Citizen* and moved to Tucson permanently. Later that year he began writing Western fiction for pulp magazines, becoming a regular contributor to *Dime Western* and *Star Western*. His first Western novel, *Gunsmoke Galoot*, appeared in 1941, and was quickly followed by *Kinkade of Red Butte* and *Boss of Panamint* in 1942. In addition to publishing novels regularly, Ernenwein continued to contribute heavily to the magazine market, both Western fiction and factual articles. Among his finest work in the 1940s are *Rebels Ride Proudly* (1947) and *Rebel Yell* (1948), both dealing with the dislocations caused by the War Between the States. In the 1950s Ernenwein wrote primarily for original paperback publishers of Western fiction because the pay was better. *High Gun* in 1956, published by Fawcett Gold Medal, won a Spur Award from the Western Writers of America, the first original paperback Western to do so. That same year, since the pulp magazine market had all but vanished, Ernenwein returned to working for the Tucson Daily Citizen, this time as a columnist. Ernenwein's Western fiction may be broadly characterized as moral allegories, light against darkness, and at the center is a protagonist determined to fight against injustice before he is destroyed by it. *Bullet Barricade* (1955), perhaps his most notable novel from the 1950s, best articulates his vision of how the life of man is not governed by a fate over which he has no control, even though life itself may seem like a never-ending contest against moral evil.